FiGHT FOR

FIGHT FOR

JUSTICE

LORI SAIGEON

Edited by Barbara Sapergia
Cover image from iStockphoto.com
Cover montage and design by Duncan Campbell
Book design by Karen Steadman
Printed and bound in Canada by Friesens

Library and Archives Canada Cataloguing in Publication

Saigeon, Lori, 1964–
    Fight for Justice / Lori Saigeon.

ISBN 978–1–55050–405–7

    I. Title.

PS8637.A448F54 2009   jC813'.6   C2009-903549-9

10 9 8 7 6 5 4 3 2

MIX
Paper from
responsible sources
FSC www.fsc.org   FSC® C016245

2517 Victoria Avenue
Regina, Saskatchewan
Canada S4P 0T2
www.coteaubooks.com

Available in Canada from:
Publishers Group Canada
2440 Viking Way
Richmond, BC V6V 1N2

The publisher gratefully acknowledges the financial support of its publishing program by: the Saskatchewan Arts Board, the Canada Council for the Arts and the Government of Canada through the Canada Book Fund.

For my children, Anna-Maria, Daniel and Michael,
who mean the world to me.
For Heather, whose unfailing love, faith
and patience sustain me.
For my students, who inspire me to write
and to keep finding quality literature for children.
For my family, especially my dad, Ed,
whose support has been invaluable over the years.
For God, Author of all of life.

I love you all.

LS

chapter 1

Justice Stoneyplain stepped out of his house and sucked in his breath. The cool air caught him by surprise. There was an autumn bite in the air of Monarch City that hadn't been there yesterday and he shivered as he shrugged into his jacket.

Justice was on his way to the Shop 'n' Go for a treat. His five-dollar allowance, fifty cents for every year of his age, was burning a hole in his pocket and he knew chips and chocolate bars were waiting for him there.

It was Saturday, Mom's "chore day." Justice was glad to be done his jobs. His twin sister, Charity, wasn't so lucky. Being a girl, she had to vacuum and wash the floors. Justice got away with doing the dishes and taking out the garbage. He knew it was easier but he never said anything to Charity and she didn't seem to mind.

Rounding the corner, Justice noticed a group of kids ahead. There were five or six boys and a couple of girls, some from his school. As he zipped his jacket up, he glanced up and down the street. It was quiet for a Saturday.

No one he knew was outside. Now he wished he did have Charity with him. She had an easy way with people and their mom said she could talk her way out of anything.

The kids huddled together, talking, but broke away from each other as he drew closer. Justice couldn't help but be reminded of a bunch of geese he saw down at Oskana Park last summer. He wondered what they could be up to so early on the weekend.

"Hey, Pretty Boy," the tallest boy called out. Trey. Justice knew him from school. Trey used to be friendly, but when he called Justice "Pretty Boy," it wasn't a sign of friendship. He was getting even for something – Justice could only guess what.

Trey came from kind of a rough family – his older brother had lots of parties at their house and the police were called there by neighbours every once in a while. Trey was athletic and fast on the playground, but Justice could pretty much keep up with him.

"I'm talking to you, Pretty Boy!" Trey spoke again, sounding loud and harsh. He looked bigger than Justice remembered, too.

"What?" Justice replied, trying to keep his voice low and steady.

"Whatcha doin'?" asked a boy Justice didn't know. Was he from another school in the neighbourhood?

"I'm just going somewhere." Justice shrugged. "I – uh, I'm kind of in a hurry."

The crowd of kids laughed together. "Oh, he's in a hurry," mimicked one of the girls. "Did his mama send him out for some milk?"

Justice almost said something back, then thought better of it. There was no sense in giving them another reason to pick on him.

As Justice edged his way through the group, somebody's foot went out and he tripped. He caught himself just before sprawling on the sidewalk. Great! That would've been the last straw – falling in front of everyone.

"Nice dance moves, Pretty Boy," giggled another girl, loud enough for him to hear. The whole group laughed. Justice felt his face flush. *I should tell them what I really think.*

"Don't be stupid," he muttered to himself. As he crossed the road toward the store, he glanced back at the crowd. They had already turned back together. *What are they doing?* Justice wondered. They seemed to have forgotten all about him, except for one boy, Jimmy, whose eyes followed Justice. When he noticed Justice looking back at him, he turned away. Justice thought he saw a sad look cross Jimmy's face. *Why would anyone stay friends with kids he doesn't like?*

Justice was relieved to reach the doors of the Shop 'n' Go and feel the warm air engulf him. Charlie, the weekend guy, was at his usual spot at the till.

"Hi, Justice," called Charlie in a friendly voice. "You're out early today. Got paid, eh?"

"Yeah," Justice chuckled. Charlie knew Justice always spent at least half his allowance every week. His mom told him he'd never save enough for a game system, but he didn't care too much. He liked his Saturday treats.

"Where's Charity?" Charlie persisted. "She don't get no treats today?"

Justice thought about Charity, at home finishing her chores and maybe setting out for here – alone. Guilt stabbed his guts.

"She's coming later," he tried to explain. "She's busy." That sounded hollow, even to Justice's own ears.

As he browsed the shelves of junk food, he wondered where she might be right now. Was she on her way already? Justice picked up a Chunky Peanut Bar and replaced it without looking at it. Charity would probably have to pass the same group of kids he'd just encountered. He glanced over the various types of nacho chips and cheese snacks. Charity might be coming out of the house right now.

Justice finally gave up trying to enjoy choosing between candy and chips, and headed for the door.

"I'll be back later, Charlie," Justice called as he shot out of the store, leaving Charlie with a puzzled look on his face.

JUSTICE COULD STILL SEE the group of kids milling around down the street. He decided to take the alley home. "I should be able to walk where I want," he mumbled. Head down, mulling over his decision, he almost ran smack into Shaunie, a girl from his class.

"Hey, Justice." Shaunie smiled, the new red streaks in her hair catching the sunlight.

"Hi," Justice muttered. He never knew what to say

to Shaunie and he could tell it wouldn't be any better this time.

"Where you goin'?" Shaunie asked.

"Home." *Very smooth,* thought Justice. *You're so cool, Pretty Boy.*

"Oh." Shaunie's smile faltered, her dark eyes losing a little of their sparkle. She seemed to have run out of things to say, too.

They stood for a moment in the crispy leaves behind someone's garage, not looking at each other. The wind whistled in Justice's ears. A moment dragged by, feeling like an hour. Shaunie kicked at something in the gravel. Justice began to feel uncomfortably hot inside his light jacket, despite the cool temperature.

"Well, I better go," he said, backing away and trying to sound as though he really had to leave.

"Okay," said Shaunie, her voice relaxing. "See you later."

"Yeah, see ya," called Justice, already metres away and moving in the other direction. A minute later he burst in the door, almost colliding with Charity on her way out.

"What's the matter?" she exclaimed.

"Nothing!" Justice sounded gruffer than he meant to.

"You look like a ghost is chasing you!"

"I'm just in a hurry. Why is everyone so surprised about that?"

"Okay, don't be so touchy! Jeez!" Charity crossed her arms and huffed. Justice pushed past her, bounded up the stairs to his room and flopped on his bed.

"Jus! Shoes!" his mom called from the living room. *How does she know?* He kicked his shoes off. Charity was right behind him.

"Aren't you going to the Shop 'n' Go?" Charity persisted, her eyebrows raised in surprise.

"Nah," he said, making his voice casual. "I'll go later. I got stuff to do."

"Okay." Charity paused for a moment before turning to go. "See you later."

"Yeah, see ya." Justice turned to the wall. Why was everything so complicated? His stomach lurched as he pictured Charity walking past Trey and the others standing around on the sidewalk.

"Charity, wait!" he called, "I'm coming with you!"

chapter 2

Justice threw on his jacket as he jogged to catch up to Charity a few houses down. "Why didn't you wait for me?" he groused.

"'Cause you're too grouchy," she replied. She tried to look angry, but Justice knew she was actually hurt. That was the thing about being a twin. It was hard to hide your feelings from each other. It made Justice hope they didn't run into Shaunie again.

"Am not," Justice argued weakly.

"Where were you before?" Charity asked. "I thought you were going to the Shop 'n' Go when you left after chores."

"Yeah, well, I changed my mind." Why did he try to lie to Charity? She would know in a second it wasn't true.

"Oh." She sounded like she wanted to say more. "Well, now you can help me carry home the bread and cheese mom wants."

Great. Now he really *was* going to shop for his

mommy. "Yeah, well, maybe I can't." *Why am I being like this?*

"Whaddya mean...?" Charity rounded on him, but stopped abruptly as they turned the corner. He didn't have a chance to answer, stopping short as he saw Shaunie at the end of the alley. She was talking to the same group of kids Justice had run into.

As Justice and Charity got within earshot of the group, one of the girls Justice didn't know suddenly shoved Shaunie on the shoulders, pushing her into another kid. Justice heard Charity suck in a quick breath.

"I'm not a loser!" Shaunie yelled. Her lips were pursed and her face looked tight. "You're the loser!" She punctuated this with a shove of her own.

The other girl's reaction was immediate. She regained her balance and pushed Shaunie back, harder. "You shut up!"

Shaunie's flushed face betrayed her feelings. The others began to egg on their friend.

"Punch her lights out, Billie!" Trey shouted. Billie – that was the girl Justice didn't know.

"Don't take that, Billie!" another girl called. Justice recognized her from school but he didn't know her name yet. She was new in the neighbourhood and not in Justice's class.

Shaunie and Billie had squared off, staring at each other, as Justice and Charity ran up to the group.

"Shaunie," Charity called, wide-eyed and breathless. "What're you doing?"

Justice glanced at Charity. She and Shaunie hung around together off and on.

Shaunie might have heard Charity but she paid no attention. Her eyes were glued to Billie.

"You guys leave her alone," Justice said. His voice sounded weak, even to himself. *Why am I so wimpy?*

"Why don't you leave us alone?" The boy Justice didn't know swung around to face Justice and Charity. "Beat it, wuss."

Justice felt his heart suddenly pick up speed. There was a muffled roaring in his ears. "Shut up." He was surprised to hear his own voice. The group turned to stare at him. *Why did I open my big mouth?* Justice wondered.

"What was that, wuss?" Trey stepped toward the twins, baring his teeth like a bear. "You're not gonna tell me what to do." The group began to circle around Justice and Charity, Shaunie and Billie forgotten.

"Just leave her alone," Justice repeated.

"Who's gonna make me?" Trey mocked. "Your mommy?" The other kids laughed – a sharp, humourless sound.

"Me," Justice surprised himself. "I'm gonna make you."

"You little snot," sneered Trey. "You'll be sorry you said that." He balled his fists and towered over Justice. Justice felt his mouth go dry. What had he done?

The sound of a car braking suddenly drew everyone's attention. Trey's head whipped around, and Justice's eyes fell on Officer Robertson's patrol car. Most of the kids knew her from her various visits to their school. They often saw her for safety presentations.

"Hey, kids!" she called cheerfully out the open passenger window. "You guys are out early for a Saturday! Everything okay?"

Relief flooded Justice's body. His knees shook and he didn't trust himself to answer.

Trey swaggered over to the officer's car, his menacing grin instantly changing to a friendly one. "Yeah, sure, Officer Robertson," he answered immediately. "Everything's great."

What a liar! Justice thought. *How can anyone change so fast?*

"Super." Officer Robertson prepared to drive off. "You guys take care, okay?"

"Okay!" the group of kids called, smiling and waving. Justice couldn't believe they were the same kids who had been threatening Shaunie and him a minute ago.

Charity took that as her cue. "Let's go," she mumbled sideways. "Come on, Shaunie." She pulled Shaunie by the arm and the three headed for the Shop 'n' Go. Justice spent the whole trip expecting Trey and his friends to be around every corner.

chapter 3

Sunday seemed to drag on and on. Justice wasn't enjoying his junk food treats. They just reminded him of the near-fight he'd had yesterday. Even the thought of heading out to the pool for their regular Sunday swim didn't excite him today.

"Jus! Chare! You guys ready to go?" Mom called up the stairs.

Justice dropped to his knees and scrabbled through the bottom drawer of his dresser for his swim stuff. "Coming, Mom!" he called back. As he yanked his trunks and towel out, a few pairs of underwear went flying.

It was a long way to the Pearson Aquatic Centre, but the swim was worth the walk on a nice day. As they strode along Wetmore Street, Charity and Mom chatted away like sisters. "We're working on a project at school," Charity was explaining to their mom. "It's about our favourite place in Canada."

"Which place did you pick," teased Mom, "the Shop 'n' Go? You go there often enough."

"No," Charity giggled. "It's supposed to be a city or a big place. We saw a movie about places in Canada and I picked Toronto. It looks so exciting!" She added, "I want to go there some day."

"Well, I hope you don't go soon, my girl," Mom replied. "It may look exciting, but it's far away and I'd miss you. Kokum and Mushum, too."

"I *know*, Mom," Charity said. "I wouldn't want to leave you guys." She paused. "Maybe I'll just visit there." She smiled and took a bouncy step.

"Good for you, Chare" Mom gave her shoulders a quick squeeze. "Don't forget where you came from." Mom looked back at Justice, slouching along a few paces behind. "How about you, Justice? Where did you pick?"

"He picked the rez!" Charity jumped in. "Why would he want to write about the reserve? It isn't new or exciting or even big!" That was the closest Charity ever came to criticizing anyone – wondering why he chose an option she didn't agree with.

"Why don't you let him tell us," Mom said gently. "I bet he knows why he picked it."

Justice felt his ears burn. "I like the rez and I want to write about it. Mr. Wilson said I could." His reason felt silly when he said it out loud, although his teacher hadn't thought so.

"That's great, Jus." Mom smiled. "You stay proud of where you're from." Justice returned her smile.

"Well *I* picked Toronto," repeated Charity. "It looks *exciting.*"

Not as exciting as the reserve, Justice thought. But he

knew it was futile to argue once Charity had made up her mind.

Warm, chlorinated air met the family at the door as they entered the Pearson Aquatic Centre. As Mom paid, Justice peeked in and saw Vance from school. *Great,* he thought, *we can hang out together.*

In less than two minutes, Justice had changed and bounded into the shallow pool. He and Vance fooled around there together, playing a keep-away game with rules they made up as they went along.

"Hey, Jus!" Vance exclaimed suddenly, "Let's go off the high board!"

Justice groaned to himself. Why did Vance have to be so brave? He was always the first kid to get onto the school roof when no adults were around and he was a daredevil with stunts on the monkey bars at recess, too. Justice loved the lower boards, but the high board looked about twelve storeys above the water. Could he even do it? And what would be worse – admitting he didn't want to, or climbing all the way up only to chicken out at the top?

Justice knocked some imaginary water out of his ears.

"C'mon, Jus, it's really cool up there!" Vance insisted. "You've been up there, right?"

Justice wondered if this was the time to be honest or to "put on a show," as his mom called it. But Vance was his friend, after all. He should be able to trust him.

"Not yet," he replied, hoping it sounded as though he just hadn't gotten around to jumping off the frightening tower.

Vance's eyes lit up. "Well, let's go then!" he shouted, pumping his fist in the air. Vance didn't seem to notice Justice's hesitation. Despite his fear, Justice chuckled at Vance – act first, think later.

Reluctantly, Justice dragged himself to the edge of the pool and pulled himself out. He tried to look enthusiastic as he approached the deep pool.

The tower loomed overhead as the two boys neared it. Again Justice wondered if he was ready for the long drop to the water. He had seen lots of kids go off the tower and it looked like an exciting freefall. That is, if someone *else* was falling, not him.

"C'mon, Jus," Vance urged again, starting up the ladder. "I'm gonna run right off!"

Not me, Justice thought. *I'll be lucky if I don't have a heart attack on the way down.* He gave himself a pep talk. *You can do this. Lots of kids do it, and they don't die. But they're not me,* he argued with himself.

"Okay, Jus, watch this!" Vance took a run and disappeared over the edge. "Woo-hoo!" he yelled on the way down.

Justice watched Vance splash into the pool and bob up a few seconds later. Other kids had started up the tower stairs behind him. He was trapped – there was no more time to think. It would be obvious if he went back down now.

Justice inched toward the edge of the tower and peered over at the water below. *Jeez, it's a long way down.* He tried not to think about it, held his nose and jumped.

A million thoughts went through his mind as he fell and yet it seemed as though he couldn't think about anything except hitting the water. He remembered to keep his legs together. His mom had told him it hurt if you didn't. Finally, yet almost instantly, he plunged into the pool. He'd made it!

Justice clawed his way to the surface to take a breath. His heart was racing. He couldn't tell if it was from the leftover fear of jumping or maybe from the excitement of still being alive. He heard Vance's voice from the edge of the pool.

"All right! Way to go! Wasn't that awesome?" Vance chattered. "Let's go again!"

Justice could hardly believe he had done it. *Wait until Mushum and Kokum hear about this. They'll be amazed,* he thought. He glanced over to where Charity and his mom were watching, and they gave him the "thumbs up." He grinned at them. Even they saw his bravery!

"Yeah, let's go!" Justice called back. He clambered out of the pool and raced Vance to the tower. His feet flew like they were on air and he wanted to jump around and yell about his achievement.

THE TWO BOYS made several more jumps until, too soon, Mom came over to the deep pool. "Justice, we've got to get going, my boy," she said. "We need some supper and I've got to get ready for work tomorrow." Reluctantly, Justice made his way to the edge of the pool.

"Van, are you staying?" he asked his friend. "The pool's pretty empty."

"Yeah, I'll go home later," Vance replied without meeting Justice's eyes. He continued to fool around at the edge of the deep pool.

"Where's your dad?" Justice persisted, careful not to mention Vance's mom, who had taken off last year to Vancouver.

"I don't know. At home," Vance answered vaguely. He suddenly seemed quiet. *Where's the kid who couldn't stop talking?* Justice wondered.

He felt funny leaving Vance at the pool alone. "Want to walk home with us?" he asked without thinking. He glanced around, looking for support from Mom. *Too late,* he thought. She was already heading into the change room, pausing only to catch his eye – *to make sure I'm going to change, too,* thought Justice.

"Yeah, okay," Vance shrugged. He swam to the edge and hauled himself out.

As the boys pushed and joked on their way to the change room, Justice couldn't believe his eyes. There were Trey and the other guys, just outside the big windows of the swimming pool building! Were they following him? He stopped and stared at them. No, they seemed to be fooling around at the side of the building. *Are they lighting matches?* Justice wondered what they could possibly be up to.

Chapter 4

As the group of four headed back up Wetmore Street, Justice's mom had a hard time keeping them moving along. *Funny how fast we went to the pool,* Justice thought. He didn't have much time to think about it because Vance was once again chattering like a monkey.

"So then I went to the Shop 'n' Go, too," he was saying. Justice's heart almost stopped. *Was that yesterday? Had Vance run into the same group of kids who had bothered him?*

"Wha'...? When did you go to the store?" Justice interrupted.

"Yesterday. Me an' Thomas. We went to the Shop 'n' Go. Trey was there." Justice's breathing quickened as he looked blankly at Vance. "You know. Trey." Vance gave Justice a puzzled look.

"Yeah, Trey," Justice repeated, his mind racing.

"Well, anyway, I got a bunch of licorice and Thomas had money for chips so we had that, too." Vance went on. "Then we went over to his house. He's got that sweet GamePlayer, you know? We played Car Crash, but I never won. You can't beat Thomas when he plays it 24/7." Vance paused. "You know?" he looked at Justice.

"Yeah," Justice nodded. He hated to ask Vance about Trey but wished he could.

They reached Vance's house. "See you tomorrow, Jus," he called as he went up the walk. The house looked dark, even though dusk was falling.

Isn't Vance's dad there? Justice wondered.

Before he thought any more about it, he heard a man's voice yelling from the darkened house. "Where have you been?"

Is that Vance's dad? Justice wondered, shocked. He sounded so different from his usual friendly self. Justice and his mom and sister stared at each other in silence. He could hear Vance's muffled reply but couldn't make out the words.

"I don't give a ——!" the man's voice nearly screamed. "Get the..." the rest of the sentence was lost as a bus rumbled by.

Then the house was silent, except for the sudden blaring of the TV. "I think we should head home," Mom said. Her voice shook a little, her eyes on Vance's house.

The rest of the walk home was quiet. Even Charity seemed subdued. When Justice looked at her, she was biting her lip.

As Justice hung up the wet swim clothes in the bath-room, he heard Mom on the phone. "No, he wasn't crying, but I could hear yelling," she was saying. *Was she talking about Vance?*

There was a pause as Mom listened to whoever was on the other end. "Yeah, Harold can get like that," she agreed with the speaker. Harold – that was Vance's dad's name. "Maybe we should call Betty." Justice wondered who Betty was. "Okay, I will." Mom seemed to have made up her mind about something. "Can I tell her what you saw last week?" she paused, waiting for an answer. "All right, but I wish *you* would."

Justice's mind raced. *What? What did the other person see that happened last week? How could there be so much going on that I don't know about?*

As Mom said goodbye and hung up the phone, Justice realized he'd better look busy. He shouldn't have been listening in on her private conversation.

Mom suddenly came up the stairs as he grabbed another towel out of the bag. "Are you still hanging up wet stuff?" she teased. "You sure move slower after swimming than before!" Justice shot her a quick look but she was smiling. He relaxed. "Come on, you can set the table."

Supper was scrambled eggs and toast. The whole family was hungry after their afternoon in the water, and eggs were the quickest to make. As they ate, Charity asked a bunch of questions. "Is Vance's dad nice, Justice? Why was he mad? Does he always yell like that? He sounded mean." "Mean" was her word for anyone who raised his voice, in contrast to Mom, who was soft-spoken – especially around others.

"I guess he's okay." Justice didn't know what to say. He had never heard Vance's dad yell like that before. He had always seemed like a pretty good guy. He had even helped Justice once when the chain from his bike came off.

"Well, I don't want to be around him," Charity stated firmly.

There was an uncomfortable silence around the table for a moment. "Hey, I got water in my ears at the pool today," Justice said suddenly.

"Maybe that's why you're moving so slowly," Mom teased. "Water in your head." Mom steered Charity onto the subject of school, her favourite place. "So tell me more about this project you guys have to do," she prompted smoothly.

And Charity was off and running. Justice let the chirping of her voice drown out the shouting of Vance's dad, still ringing in his ears.

chapter 5

Jus! Chare! Breakfast is on!" Mom called up the stairs. "Let's get going!"

Reluctantly, Justice sat up and pulled on his jeans and T-shirt, still strewn on his bed. Why was it so much easier to get up on the weekend? He was still yawning as Charity danced into the room.

"Look, Jus, Mom braided my hair!" She twirled around Justice's bedroom so he could have a better look. "Look!" she practically shouted, her voice sparkling with excitement.

"Yeah, it's great," Justice said without much enthusiasm. It was just braids. How could girls get so wrapped up in their looks?

"Oh, I *love* when my hair is braided!" Charity exclaimed, flouncing out.

As the kids ate, Mom bustled around the kitchen making lunches. "Can you cut up some tomatoes after school for burgers?" she asked.

"Sure, Mom," Charity answered immediately. Her good mood obviously extended to everyone and everything.

Justice silently nibbled his toast. Mom and Charity continued to chatter until Mom said she had to run. She worked at the Circle of Colours Health Centre and she had to be there by 8:00 AM.

"You kids be good today. Don't forget to lock up," she reminded them, as she did every day. "Love you both." She leaned over to kiss Justice and he offered his cheek. She chuckled and shook her head as she gave him a hug. "I'll see you around 5:30."

"Bye, Mom!" Charity called from halfway up the stairs. "Have a good day!"

Justice watched as his mom hurried down the walk and turned in the direction of the Circle of Colours. She pulled her jacket tighter as she crossed the street. *It must be colder out today than it was yesterday,* he thought. *Winter is coming.*

Nearly an hour later, Justice and Charity were picking up their backpacks and heading out the door.

"Justice," Charity said, "isn't that Vance?"

"Vance!" Justice called. "Wait for me!" Vance didn't seem to hear him.

"Vance!" Justice called louder. "Wait!"

Justice caught up with Vance. "Hey," he greeted.

"Hey," Vance finally replied.

Justice suddenly felt uncomfortable. "Cold out, eh?" he said lamely.

"Yup," Vance answered back without looking up. Justice noticed that Vance's thin spring coat was only half done up; some of the snaps were missing. *He must be pretty cold.*

The two boys walked in silence until they neared the grounds of McTavish School. "Hey, that was fun at the pool yesterday, Van," Justice said.

"Yup," Vance said as he jogged toward the climbing apparatus. He chucked down his backpack. It hit the school fence as he leaped up to the horizontal bar at one end. Vance easily swung himself up and climbed along the metal bars. Justice thought he seemed more monkey than boy. He watched Vance for a few seconds then decided to find someone more interested in talking to him.

The morning passed by quickly. The announcement for an upcoming "Pyjama Day" caused a small excitement in the classroom. Justice wondered what he would wear, considering that he slept in his underwear only. He wasn't too worried about it, though. He was getting too old for school spirit days, anyway.

After the lunch bell rang, Justice noticed Charity heading for the school door with her coat on. She was with her best friend, Dani. "Charity!" he called to her, "Where are you going?"

"We're going to O.K." Charity answered flippantly. "See ya."

"Open Kitchen? But we brought lunch," Justice persisted. It wasn't like Charity to just disobey their mom like this. *Is she trying to act more grown up than she should because of her friend?* Justice wondered.

"I know, but Dani wants me to go and I'm going," Charity turned, ending the conversation. Justice thought she looked a little unsure about going and didn't want to keep talking about it. *Maybe she's afraid she'll change her mind,* he thought.

Justice didn't want to argue with her. Still, he didn't think Mom would want Charity to go. Open Kitchen was a free lunch program for kids in their neighbourhood, but it was quite a long walk and Mom didn't want the twins to leave the school building. For some reason Mom seemed to think O.K. was only for kids who didn't have enough food at home. She was pretty upset when Justice went to Open Kitchen one time last year. *Oh well,* thought Justice, *Charity is a whole year older now; maybe Mom won't mind.* Justice saw Vance with a big group of kids heading that way, too.

Still, the nagging feeling of something not quite right bothered him while he ate his sandwich. The only good thing was that Jimmy stayed for lunch and Justice ate with him. They talked about going to the pool together one day. It turned out Jimmy had never been off the high board, either. *You should go there with Vance,* Justice thought. *Then you'd go off the high board!*

The lunchroom was loud, especially with all the younger kids chatting and giggling. *Maybe I should have gone to O.K., too,* Justice grumbled to himself. *I'm getting too old to sit here with a lunchroom babysitter.*

chapter 6

By the time school began for the afternoon, Justice knew something was wrong. Charity hadn't returned from Open Kitchen. It was unlike her to be late for school. As their teacher, Mr. Wilson, took attendance, he glanced at Justice. "Do you know where Charity is?" he asked.

Justice wasn't sure what to say. He didn't really know where Charity was but he had a pretty good idea. "Uh, she, uh, went to O.K. for lunch," he mumbled.

"Oh," Mr. Wilson looked surprised. "Didn't you go?"

"No." Justice would have said more, but the whole class was watching. He waited for Mr. Wilson to move on. Mr. Wilson continued with attendance. "Billie? She was here this morning, too. Janet, you're here. Mr. Wilson clapped the book shut. "Okay, that's everyone."

No sooner had the attendance book been sent down to the office than Mrs. Lipswitch, the school secretary, called over the intercom. "Excuse me, Mr. Wilson?"

"Yes?" he raised his voice to be heard on the old system.

"Is Justice Stoneyplain in class? You have him marked here, but Charity is marked absent," the crackly voice continued.

"Yes, he's here, but she's not," Mr. Wilson confirmed.

"All right, thank you," she replied.

Justice couldn't keep his mind on math, wondering where Charity was. His unasked questions were soon answered; Mrs. Lipswitch was back on the intercom. "Pardon the interruption, Mr. Wilson," she said. "Can you send Justice down to the office, please?"

"He's on his way," answered Mr. Wilson, indicating the door. "Go ahead, Justice."

Justice shot out of the room, sweat breaking out all over him. *This must be about Charity,* he thought. His heart pounded in his ears. He made it to the office in record time.

"Mr. Baker is waiting for you, Justice," Mrs. Lipswitch tilted her head toward the principal's office door, her hands never leaving her computer. "Just knock and go on in."

Justice knocked on the door as he opened it.

"Come on in, Justice," said Mr. Baker. Two figures were seated at the conference table. One was Dani, looking subdued and pale, and the other was Charity. The right side of her face was scraped and tears still wet her cheeks. Her eyes looked puffy; she had obviously been crying for a while.

"Charity?" he blurted, his voice shaking. Charity didn't say anything, but fresh tears ran down her cheeks.

Mr. Baker began. "Justice, do you know what happened today?"

"No," Justice muttered, his mind racing. *What* had *happened?*

Mr. Baker continued. "Charity and Dani say there was some trouble at O.K. Do you know anything about it?"

Justice felt guilt clutch at his stomach – he shouldn't have let her go – but he was also angry at Charity. *Why did she have to go to Open Kitchen in the first place?*

"No, I wasn't there," he said.

Ms. Fayant, a teachers' assistant, opened the door. "Here, Charity, put this ice pack on your face. It'll feel better if you numb it a bit."

"Thanks," Charity mumbled.

"So, Charity," Mr. Baker began, "tell me again what happened."

"We were leaving O.K. and these kids started bugging us." Charity's words were quiet, the ice pack pressed against her cheek.

"We weren't even doing anything!" interrupted Dani. She sat up in her chair and her face flushed. "They just started calling Charity names for no reason!" her voice grew louder as she talked.

Mr. Baker held up his hand. "I want to hear from Charity now, please," he said. "You've had your turn, Dani."

He turned back to Charity. "Go on."

Charity took a deep breath and it whooshed out with a sudden drop of her shoulders. She swallowed hard. "So we were starting back towards the school and these kids started calling me names and pushing us around." Her lower lip trembled. "Then when Dani tried to tell them to leave me alone, one of them pushed me down. That's how...how..." she faltered, then drew in a ragged breath. "That's how I scraped my face," she finished in a rush.

"Do you know who any of those kids were?" asked their principal.

"No," Charity answered without looking up.

Justice knew instantly that she was lying. *Why would she lie to the principal, at school?* he wondered, shocked. *Charity isn't usually like that.*

Mr. Baker must have sensed that something didn't add up as well. "Didn't you recognize even one of the kids?" he persisted. "Maybe you've seen them around, even if they don't go to our school."

"No, I don't know them," Charity repeated.

Justice's mind raced. She must have *some* good reason for not telling the truth, but he couldn't think of anything except that she must be afraid to tell Mr. Baker who the kids were. "Maybe they're from Garnet School," he suggested, trying to sound helpful.

Mr. Baker was not so easily diverted. "Seems odd that they would be walking towards McTavish School, though, doesn't it?" he asked.

An awkward silence followed. Justice couldn't stand the uncomfortable pause. "Chare, are you okay?"

"Yeah," she answered, her voice still shaky. Justice knew she *wasn't* okay, but she didn't want to say any more in front of their principal.

Mr. Baker seemed to decide that the conversation was over. "Dani, you can head up to class now," he said. "Justice, you and Charity take another few minutes and when she feels better you can go back to class, too."

"Okay, thanks, Mr. Baker," Justice replied.

The principal went out, leaving the door open. "I'm going up to Mrs. Wernichuk's room," he informed the secretary. "There seems to be some kids missing from there, too."

Justice sank into a chair near Charity. "Are you really okay, Chare?" he asked, gently placing a hand on her shoulder.

"No," her muffled voice came from where she had her head down on her arms. Justice waited for a few minutes while she cried quietly. As her breathing slowed, she lifted her head and placed the ice pack against her cheek again.

"What happened, really?" Justice asked.

"Tell you later," was all Charity would say, glancing out the open door toward where Mrs. Lipswitch was now on the phone.

They sat for a few moments in silence, until Charity stood up. "Let's go to class," she said, her voice controlled and dull.

Justice followed her in silence, a million questions burning his mind. As they passed through the office door and headed for the stairs, he tried again. "What really happened?"

"Oh, Jus, it was Trey and those kids from the street on Saturday!" Charity whispered fiercely. "They all circled around us and started calling me bad names and they said Pretty Boy couldn't help me, and...and..." Charity faltered. "What have they got against you?"

"I don't know," Justice muttered through gritted teeth, "but they can't get away with this!" He shoved the classroom door open.

The rest of the afternoon dragged by. Justice couldn't keep his mind on school work. It seemed so pointless to worry about multiplication and the capitals of the provinces when his sister had been threatened and hurt. Every time he thought about the incident, his blood boiled.

chapter 7

By the time Justice and Charity walked in the door after school, they were both tired from the long afternoon. Charity had spent recess trying to explain to her friends what had happened without really telling them anything, and Justice had spent it trying to avoid hearing the story over and over.

"What are you going to tell Mom?" Justice asked her as he got a box of cookies down from the cupboard.

"I dunno. She'll be mad if she finds out I went to O.K."

"You better tell her something. She's gonna see the scrapes on your face," he pointed out.

"Maybe I should tell her what really happened," Charity said.

"Maybe you better tell her you fell," Justice suggested. "She might decide to call Trey's mom or Billie's mom. You don't want her getting them in trouble and making it worse for you."

"I could tell her I got pushed down playing soccer. That's partly true," Charity mused.

"Good idea."

The instant Mom walked in the door after work the look on her face told them they wouldn't need to explain. She strode over to where Charity was flaked out on the couch watching TV. Mom sat down next to Charity without even taking off her coat.

"Chare, what happened today?" she asked, her voice tight. "Let me see your face."

"It was nothing, Mom, I just fell down." Charity avoided Mom's intense eyes. "It's okay now."

"I've been worried sick since Mr. Baker called me after lunch. He said you had trouble with some kids coming back from Open Kitchen –" She broke off, waiting for an answer.

"Mom, I just wanted to go for once," Charity began. "Dani always goes to O.K. and she said it was lots of fun." Charity's eyes pleaded for their mom to understand.

"Honey, I know you'd like to go to Open Kitchen with your friends sometimes, but I just feel it's safer for you to eat at school. We've been through this before, and now I guess you know why I feel this way." Mom stopped her explanation.

"So now I'll never get to go again," Charity said. Justice didn't think Charity would want to go again after today anyway.

Mom sighed. "You don't need to go, my girl. We can afford lunch every day, and I like to know you have an adult supervising you. Remember, you're still only ten."

Only ten. Justice turned back to the TV, his mind racing. *I may be "only ten," but I can look after myself. And my sister,* he added to himself. His breath quickened and his heart raced again as the cartoon pictures on the screen were replaced in his mind by the images he had of that group of kids swarming his sister.

Next time, I'll be there, he vowed.

LATER THAT EVENING, the family's phone rang. Charity ran to pick it up, as usual. "Hi, Kokum!" she said brightly. Justice perked up as he tried to figure out the conversation from just one side.

"Yeah, school's fine," she said. "We're doing a really cool project," she continued. "I'm writing about Toronto!"

There was a pause as their grandma responded.

"Yup, I *always* do my best," Charity stated proudly. She listened again. "Yeah, Jus is right here." She handed the phone to Justice. "Kokum wants to say hi," she told him.

"Hi, Kokum," Justice said into the phone.

"Justice! How's my boy?" Kokum asked. Justice could hear the smile in her voice. He pictured Kokum sitting at the table in her small, neat kitchen. He could almost see the view of open space out her window and smell the bannock she might have baked that day.

"I'm good, Kokum, how about you and Mushum?" Justice replied.

Kokum chuckled. "Oh, your mushum is out in the shed getting his hands greasy in that nasty snowmobile motor," she answered. "He is convinced he can make it run *all* winter this year."

Justice laughed. "Well, that would be the first time!" he said.

"When are you kids coming out to see us?" Kokum asked.

"I dunno," replied Justice. "I'll ask Mom." He turned to his mom, who was scooping muffin mix into pans. "Mom, Kokum wants to know when we're coming out."

"Let me talk to her, please," said his mom in reply.

Justice hung around, also waiting for the answer.

"Hi, Mom, it's me," Justice's mom said into the phone after she had wiped off her hands. "Well, I was just thinking about coming out pretty soon. I don't want to wait until there's a blizzard before we get out there again." She paused. "She's back? How is she?" And Mom and Kokum were off and running, talking about people Justice didn't know from the reserve where his mom grew up.

Justice knew the two women would be gabbing for a while, so he went back to watching TV, restlessly waiting to find out when his family would be together again.

Things would be so much easier if I just lived on the reserve with Kokum and Mushum.

chapter 8

t 7:00 the next morning, Justice pulled himself out of a deep sleep as Mom called for the kids to get up. The memory of what happened to Charity at O.K. yesterday rushed back to him like a river, with him caught in the currents. He lay in bed for a few minutes before he felt he could face the day. He didn't know what he was going to do to help Charity, but he knew he was going to defend her in some way.

Their mom's usual cheerfulness seemed dampened this morning. Despite Justice's bleary morning eyes, he noticed that lines of worry crossed his mom's face and her mouth looked drawn where a smile usually played on her lips.

Charity came into the kitchen quietly. She looked ready for school except for her bouncy step. Justice felt angry all over again. *No way can those kids do this to us!* he thought. *I'm gonna do something about it!*

"Charity, I don't know who those kids are," Mom said, "but I want you to stay away from them.

Whatever is bugging them is their problem, not yours."

That was Mom's philosophy – don't make somebody else's problems your problems – not if you can help it. Mom was a peacemaker. He just didn't know if that was the answer all the time. She didn't have to live at school with these kids. Of course, she didn't know that some of these kids were at the same school as Charity and Justice. She really didn't know much about the whole thing; Charity had decided to keep quiet about most of it.

"I know, Mom." Charity was also a peacemaker. She didn't want to upset Mom, and Justice knew she would stay as far from those kids as possible.

I, on the other hand, he told himself, *I am the man of the house, and I have to look after the others in my own way.*

"MY FACE LOOKS TERRIBLE!" Charity groaned later as she peered into the bathroom mirror. "I'm gonna use some of Mom's make-up to cover up the scrapes."

"Come on, Chare," Justice said after a few minutes. He was glad he wasn't a girl, worried about how he looked all the time. It was odd for him to be urging her to get to school on time – it was usually the other way around. "We better get going," he said again, glancing at the clock.

As the siblings hit the sidewalk, a blast of cold air grabbed their jackets. Justice wished he'd worn gloves.

"I wonder if it's going to snow," he said. "It sure feels cold out."

Charity looked around. "Maybe." She shrugged her shoulders carelessly.

Nearing the school, Justice was glad it was almost time to go into class. Even his feet felt the cold through his runners. He was sure snow was coming. He hoped there would be lots. That would mean snowmobiling out at the reserve, whenever they could get out there. He longed to leave behind the grimy city and the bullying kids, and feel the freedom of the wide-open space at Mushum and Kokum's house.

Children jostled for a spot in the lineup until Ms. Fayant, the supervisor, blew her whistle at them. "Okay, stop pushing," she called. "Line up before someone gets hurt." The kids mostly obeyed her. As Justice and Vance joked around and elbowed each other, Justice noticed Trey and his buddies approaching the line. Trey had on that smug grin he seemed to wear a lot and Justice felt his own temperature rising again. Fortunately the bell rang and the line began to move ahead.

As the kids settled into class, Justice relaxed a little. He really liked Mr. Wilson. They did some cool things in Language Arts, which was first in the day. Right now they were reading an adventure novel, and the kids took parts they liked and acted them out. Justice didn't like the acting much, but Vance made a good shipwrecked kid. What an actor he was, and it was a great story. Justice lost himself in wondering how the boy in the story would get out of his latest encounter, this time with a wild animal on the island.

JUSTICE WAS AMAZED when it was nearly recess time and Mr. Wilson was calling for books and other materials to be put away. That was one power Justice caved in to – the power of a good story to take you away.

As the kids burst out of the doors onto the playground, Justice grinned to himself. He had been right about the weather. The ground was covered with a thin layer of white. *I'm getting like an old mushum,* he thought proudly. *Pretty soon I'll be tracking rabbits, too.*

Justice's thoughts about the ways he was like Mushum were interrupted by someone bumping hard into his shoulder and he almost fell into Vance. He turned to say, "Watch it," but realized that the person who had smashed into him was Chelsie, a new girl from another class. She was looking back over her other shoulder, not at him. As he followed her gaze, he spied Trey. *Who else?*

"Don't hurt Pretty Boy," Trey was laughing without humour. "He gets upset when girls try to beat him up." His voice was edged with scorn. As Justice glared at him, Trey made a rude gesture, turned and walked away. At that moment, Justice felt as though he had been walking on twigs and the last one had just broken. His heart suddenly raced and his face flushed with heat. Everything else dropped away and he could only see Trey's retreating back.

Justice heard nothing but a roaring in his ears as he rushed at Trey and shoved him, hard. Trey was knocked off balance and stumbled for a few steps. He managed to stay on his feet and turned at the same time. Trey cursed.

"What's the matter with you?" he growled, his voice tight and his teeth clenched.

"Leave me and my sister alone," Justice warned, his voice barely in control.

Trey sneered. "I do what I want."

"No, you don't," Justice persisted, his hands balling up into fists. A crowd of kids was beginning to gather, but Justice didn't notice.

"Listen, Pretty Boy," Trey spat at Justice, "a little wuss like you doesn't tell me what to do." He had moved closer to Justice as he spoke and was now only an arm's length in front of him. "So shut up." Trey punctuated this last statement with a shove on Justice's shoulders.

This time Justice was ready for him and met his shove with another of his own. Trey's eyebrows registered surprise for a second and then drew together in anger. Before Justice even realized what was happening, Trey was rushing at him and had hold of his jacket.

Around them, kids were yelling. "Get him!" some were shouting.

"Fight! Fight! Fight!"

Trey's buddies were urging him on, "You get him, Trey!"

"Punch him out!"

Justice didn't hear any of them over the roar in his ears. He began swinging wildly in Trey's direction and before he knew it they both went down, Trey on top.

Suddenly Trey flew off Justice before either of them could get in a decent hit. Ms. Fayant was there, holding Trey and shouting for Justice to get up. "Get to the office, both of you," she was saying loudly and firmly. There was no arguing with Ms. Fayant. She could be as tough as she was funny. Her usually smiling face was not smiling right now and Justice obeyed her immediately. Trey shook her hands off his jacket.

"Trey, get to the office," she repeated.

Justice could hardly think as he headed in the direction of the door. He wiped snot from under his nose and tried to catch his breath. His heart was still racing but the jet engine sound in his ears was beginning to fade. Trey came up beside him, Ms. Fayant right behind.

"You're dead, Pretty Boy," Trey hissed.

"Never mind that, Trey," broke in Ms. Fayant. "Just keep walking."

chapter 9

Justice's mind was spinning with thoughts, none of them clear. *Trey better not hurt my sister...Trey could hurt me if he wanted to...I'm in trouble because of Trey. I am the man of the house....*

Both boys threw themselves into chairs by the office while Ms. Fayant went in. Trey's icy looks upset Justice, but he tried hard not to show it.

Soon Mr. Baker emerged from his office. His normally friendly, caring face looked tight and upset. "Trey, Justice, come in here," he commanded quietly.

He led them in, indicating the same table where Justice had sat when Charity was hurt. "Why don't you sit down?" he suggested but he was really leaving the boys no choice.

Surprisingly, Mr. Baker sat down at his own desk. "You boys cool off for a few minutes while I finish this report," he said calmly, turning to his computer. "Get your thoughts together."

Justice wasn't quite sure what Mr. Baker meant but

he tried to sort out his feelings. As his anger subsided, he began to think about what had happened outside. He realized that Trey had been trying to start a fight and that he, Justice, had jumped right in. Justice admitted it to himself; he had been waiting to even the score with Trey. This had been a great opportunity. Justice knew that the fight looked like Trey's fault, though. He considered what that might mean for him.

Before he had everything figured out, Mr. Baker had risen and was joining the boys at the table. He had a notebook and pen in his hands. "So let's find out what went wrong out there, okay?" Mr. Baker turned to Justice. "Justice, tell me your side of the story."

My side of the story? thought Justice. *I'd like to tell you what Trey is really like.* "I was coming out the door for recess and Trey just shoved Chelsie into me," he began.

"I did not!" interrupted Trey. "I wasn't even near them!"

"Trey, hold on, please," Mr. Baker held out a hand in a gesture that reminded Justice of a police officer stopping traffic. "You'll have your say next." He turned back to Justice. "Go on," he urged.

"Well, Trey pushed Chelsie, and she bumped into me." Justice tried to ignore the glares Trey was shooting across the table. For a moment, he faltered. "At least, I think that's what happened," Justice hesitated again. He was losing his nerve. "Then we started fighting." Justice felt caged, like a tiger that couldn't get out. It wasn't really what he wanted to say, but it was so hard when Trey was staring at him.

"Okay," Mr. Baker paused for a moment, looking hard at Justice, then made some notes. Justice wondered what he was writing. "Trey, how about you?"

Trey leaned forward in his chair. He didn't look worried, he actually looked – what was the word – honest? "I was just coming out for recess, Mr. Baker," Trey began, turning wide eyes toward the principal, "and Justice started yelling at me." Trey's voice held surprise and indignation. "I don't know what's got into him." He turned to Justice. "Why are you such a jerk, anyway?"

"Trey," Mr. Baker warned, "watch it."

"Oh, sorry, Mr. Baker," Trey replied.

"So, Trey, you don't know how this fight started?" Mr. Baker asked.

"Well, Justice is really mad and I don't know why," Trey replied. Justice couldn't believe his ears. *How could Trey put such a spin on things? And where did he learn to do that? His big brother?*

"Justice?" Mr. Baker turned back to him. "Is this true?"

Was he really mad? Of course he was mad! Trey had been picking on him and Charity for a while now. Yes, he was mad about it! How could Justice explain all these little things to Mr. Baker? If you said them out loud, they wouldn't sound like anything.

"Well, he shoved Chelsie into me," Justice repeated as an answer. Suddenly this didn't look so much like Trey's fault. "He started it." Justice finished lamely.

Mr. Baker looked silently from one boy to the other.

"It sounds to me like you two were just waiting to fight each other," he concluded. "I wonder why."

Should he tell Mr. Baker that Trey was one of the kids who bullied Charity at O.K.? *That might make things worse with Trey,* he told himself.

"You boys are going to have to do some work for the caretaker at afternoon recess today. That should keep you too busy to fight." Mr. Baker said. "Trey, since this is your second fight in the last while, I'm going to have to phone your parents. Both of you – report to Mrs. McDonald at recess. She'll have a job for you. Get along. Do your best."

Great, thought Justice, *now I'm in trouble and have to work, all because of Trey. I'll get you back,* he thought. He felt ugly inside and oddly comforted at the same time.

MOVING CHAIRS at recess time should have worked off some of Justice's anger, but his blood still boiled every time he looked at Trey and thought about their fight.

It wasn't fair! Trey started it, and yet he, Justice, got just as much blame. What was worse, Trey acted helpful to Mrs. McDonald, the caretaker, earning himself praise. Of course Trey grinned smugly at Justice over that, too.

You'll get yours, Justice thought, *just wait.* Justice didn't know how he would pay Trey back but he knew he would do it somehow.

chapter 10

The rest of the week went more smoothly for Justice. School continued as usual. Trey missed a couple of days of school and seemed to keep out of Justice's way when he was there – at least for now. Justice tried to ignore the fact that Trey was even on the playground, although he noticed a few scuffles where Trey seemed to be involved just until an adult became aware. That's when he suddenly vanished and the supervisors spoke to the other kids.

By Saturday morning, Justice was hurrying through his chores again and allowing his mouth to water over the thought of chips and candy bars. His daydreams were interrupted by Charity's quiet voice. He listened immediately, since it was so rare for her not to be chattering at him.

"Jus, are you going to the Shop 'n' Go pretty soon?" she murmured.

"Yeah, why?" he replied.

She glanced around as she spoke, "'Cause, can you get me something?"

Right, she's grounded because of going to Open Kitchen without permission, he remembered.

"Chare, I'm gonna get in trouble," he complained.

"Oh, come on, I won't have any candy all week if you don't," she begged.

Justice imagined all week without a treat. "All right," he relented, "what do you want? And you better have the money for it."

"I do, I do," Charity promised, her face beaming. She ran to get her money as Justice wondered what had happened to the girl who would never disobey their mom.

THE WIND WHISTLED in Justice's ears and cut through his jacket as he headed down the street to the Shop 'n' Go. It really was turning colder now; blizzards with lots of snow couldn't be far away. Justice shoved his hands in his pockets. Winter meant no more bike riding, but Justice didn't care. His bike frame was bent and Mom said she wouldn't take it to be fixed until spring. Besides, winter also meant snowmobiling on the reserve and Justice could hardly wait. He loved the feeling of power that revving the motor gave him. His mushum had taught him to drive on his own last winter and he could hardly wait for that freedom again.

Before he knew it, the Shop 'n' Go appeared ahead. Justice had been so busy thinking that the city blocks had slipped by him unnoticed.

As JUSTICE PUSHED OPEN THE DOOR, he was surprised to see a stranger at the till. *Where's Charlie, the regular weekend guy?* he wondered. The new clerk glanced up from a magazine as Justice entered the store and then went back to reading.

Justice headed for the chips first. He knew he would be buying Crispy Nacho Chipos and he prepared to enjoy choosing which flavour. While he decided between "extra spicy" and "extra cheesy," the bell at the door announced another customer. Justice and the clerk looked up at the same time.

Justice felt his heart start to pound. It was one of the boys he'd seen with Trey on the street last Saturday! He definitely did not go to Justice's school, but Justice had seen him around before. Justice didn't think the boy had seen him and he wondered if he should make his way out the door.

Too late! The boy was headed toward him. As the boy rounded the shelf where the chips were, he caught sight of Justice and sneered.

"Pretty Boy," he hissed. "Stay outta my way."

So now he's *using my "nickname" – great.* Justice steamed at Trey all over again. Justice decided to stay where he was and tried to keep looking for his chips. He couldn't help but notice the boy's runners. They were covered with strange symbols someone had written on with pen. Justice wondered what they were for. They looked oddly familiar, but he couldn't place them. Then with a shock he remembered seeing the same signs spray-painted on garbage cans and garage doors. *Gang symbols?*

"I said get lost," the boy snapped at Justice.

Justice chose his chips and moved away to look at chocolate bars. The boy trailed after him a minute later. He glared at Justice again but said nothing more.

Both boys glanced up as another customer entered the store. It was a man Justice didn't know. He began asking directions, complaining about the "ridiculous number of one-way streets" in the city. The clerk slid his magazine aside with a sigh and began indicating things on the man's map.

As Justice turned back to the racks of candy, he noticed the other boy's jacket pocket gaping open. He could just imagine sliding a chocolate bar into it, making it look as though the boy was trying to steal it. He knew the boy would be in trouble if he were caught, maybe even with the police. *What a great payback that would be for last weekend,* he thought.

Justice glanced back at the till. The two men were still gesturing and naming streets. Justice grabbed a chocolate bar, fingering it. Suddenly, the other boy reached up for a small bag for loose candy. Without thinking about it again, Justice popped the bar into the boy's open pocket.

In a split second, Justice had turned back to the racks of candy, his heart pounding. The other boy was busy crinkling open his bag in preparation to filling it. Justice's face was hot and he was so dizzy he could hardly concentrate on the bars in front of him. He grabbed the first one he could and turned to head for the till.

"What's going on there?" called the clerk, his attention suddenly on the boys. Justice's head whipped in the direction of his voice. The stranger was gone. Justice hadn't even noticed the bell on the door ring when he'd left. *What had the clerk seen?*

"Nothing," Justice replied, his voice trembling slightly. The other boy just stood in silence, his mouth slightly open, his hand halfway in the bag of candy.

"I saw you put something in his pocket," the clerk said, indicating the other boy. Instantly the boy searched his pockets, coming out with the chocolate bar.

The other boy's eyes widened. "This isn't mine!" he declared, holding it out in one hand as though it were on fire. Justice could hardly breathe.

"You two stay right there," the clerk commanded, pointing at the boys, coming out from behind the counter and approaching them. The other boy's eyes slid toward the door. Justice wondered if he might try to run. "Now what's going on here?" the clerk demanded, "I saw you two talking to each other."

"I don't even know this stupid kid," the boy growled. "Why'd you put this in my pocket?" he spat at Justice.

"I saw you talking to him," the clerk repeated. He hesitated. "I'm calling your parents."

"We don't have a phone," the other boy sneered.

That seemed to take the clerk aback. "What about you?" he said, turning to Justice.

Justice was too shocked to lie, even if he wanted to. "We do," he answered, looking down.

"All right, then," the clerk huffed. He seemed satisfied with that. "You," he turned to the other boy, "I don't want to see you in here for at least a week. And you," he pointed at Justice, "come with me to the phone at the till. We're calling your home."

Justice slouched up to the front of the store while the other kid dumped his candy at the till and headed out the door. He looked back as he pushed the door open and mouthed to Justice, "You're dead."

How could you be so stupid? Justice berated himself. *Now you're in trouble and he's not!* He wished he could relive the last ten minutes and change the way things had turned out.

The clerk was looking at him expectantly, his hand on the phone. "Well, what is it?" he asked.

"What?" Justice asked, not following.

"I said, what's your phone number?" the clerk repeated, raising his voice.

"Oh," Justice replied and recited the digits, his heart sinking with each push of a button. He couldn't imagine what his mom would say.

"Hello, I'm calling from the Shop 'n' Go," the clerk said into the phone. "Is your mom home?" Charity must have answered. "Yes, hello, I'm calling from the Shop 'n' Go," he repeated. "I think I have your son here." He covered the receiver and turned to Justice. "What's your name, kid?"

"Justice," he mumbled, wishing he were somewhere else.

"I have Justice here," he continued. "Could you

please come and get him?" He paused. "No, he's fine, but you better come and get him anyway." Justice could hear his mom's voice, but couldn't make out her words. "Okay, we'll wait here."

chapter 11

T he minutes dragged by as Justice stood there uncomfortably, waiting for his mom. A few people entered the store, glancing curiously at him, then made their purchases and left. He could hardly think about what Mom might say. Never before had he tried something so stupid. *And the other kid got away!* Justice felt sick as he imagined what would happen to him.

His mom soon arrived, breathless and dishevelled. Charity was right behind her.

"Justice, what's going on here?" she asked the moment she came through the Shop 'n' Go door.

"Are you this boy's mom?" the clerk asked curtly.

"Yes, did you call me?" Mom turned to the clerk, her face flushed and her eyebrows drawn together.

"Yeah, I did," the clerk replied, glancing from one to the other. "Your son put a chocolate bar into his buddy's pocket. I don't know what he's trying to pull over on me but I think they were trying to steal it."

Charity's mouth dropped open.

"What?" Mom's eyes widened. "Justice, is this true?"

Justice looked from one to the other, his throat so tight he could barely swallow. "Yeah."

Mom's face flushed a little deeper and her mouth tightened into a line. After a moment she turned to the clerk. "I'm really sorry about this. I'm not sure what Justice was doing, but he doesn't usually do this. Can I pay for the chocolate bar?" she asked.

"No, it's all right," the clerk nodded, his face relaxing slightly. "The other kid left it here. Just make sure your son doesn't come back in here without you for a while."

"Of course." Mom turned to Justice. "Come home with us now," she stated flatly. Charity fell in beside Justice, her eyes searching his face. The three left the store.

Justice was amazed to notice the wind still whistling outside, the sun still in its regular place in the sky. Nothing out here had changed, yet he felt completely different. He could hardly stand to know what his mom thought about him.

The family trudged half a block in silence. Mom's back looked stiff and she stared in the direction of home as she led the way.

Finally, after what seemed forever, she turned to Justice. "What do you think you were doing in that store?" she asked, her voice unusually loud and harsh.

"Mom, I don't really know that guy. He's not my friend," Justice began to explain.

"What do you mean, you don't know him? The clerk said you were talking to each other and you gave him a chocolate bar," Mom repeated what she had been told.

"No, *he* was talking to *me,*" Justice said and told her the story of what had happened at the Shop 'n' Go.

Mom stared at Justice for the length of a few houses. "But why? Why would you do something like that?"

Justice looked at the ground, then back at his mom, who waited expectantly.

"I – I don't know," he finally said, wondering if that was enough of an answer.

"Justice, how could you DO that?" Charity finally found her voice. "You were stealing!"

"Look, it just happened, I don't know why, okay?" Justice could feel his face getting hot. He wanted to say more, to explain, but his eyes were suddenly stinging and he didn't trust his voice.

"Justice, this just isn't like you," Mom said, looking down and shaking her head. "I can't understand what you were trying to do. You have embarrassed our family. Now Charity can't go to the Shop 'n' Go, *I* can't go to the Shop 'n' Go, without the clerk knowing we are all part of your family. We don't behave this way. What we need, we buy. It's always been this way. You understand that, don't you?"

Mom rarely gave such long speeches. Justice knew she was serious.

"Yeah, I know." There was little else he could say. How could he describe the nasty feeling of revenge he'd had when he saw the other boy? He felt sick all over again, just reliving the events in the store.

"You are grounded from the Shop 'n' Go for a month. I don't know what else to do with you," Mom said, her voice stern and sad.

The rest of the walk seemed longer than usual as the three carried on in silence. Even Charity seemed at a loss for words. Finally they reached home. Justice went straight to his room without a word to the others. His mind was in turmoil as he sat at his table and fiddled uselessly with his school project.

EVENTUALLY THERE WAS A TAP at his door and Mom came in. "Justice, I want to talk to you." Her usually pleasant voice held no life. "Come here," she indicated Justice's bed as she sat down.

He came away from the table and sat down by his mom, his eyes downcast.

"I'm not sure what happened in that store but I want you to know I meant what I said," she began. "Do you know what was wrong in what you did?"

"Yeah, but you don't understand," Justice burst out.

"Maybe I don't, but I understand what is right and wrong, Jus, and you do, too," Mom pointed out.

"I know," Justice huffed. How could he tell his mom what had been going on for the last while at school and in the neighbourhood? He would probably be getting Charity in trouble for lying to Mr. Baker and not telling Mom everything, and his mom would know he had been covering up. "I know," he repeated.

There was a long pause while Mom seemed to decide something. "Look, we're going out to Kokum and Mushum's next weekend. I want you at home all the time you're not in school until we go out to the reserve, understand?"

"Yeah." Justice was surprised his mom didn't punish him further for the incident. Maybe she still would.

The next week dragged by. Justice walked to and from school, always expecting the kid from the Shop 'n' Go to jump out at him from every alley and doorway. He wondered daily what had happened to him and was thankful many times that the other boy went to a different school. Justice was glad to have an excuse for having to go straight home. He didn't really want to hang around the schoolyard with that guy around. He didn't want to run into Trey, either. Except for the walks back and forth to school, Justice felt as though he'd never see the outdoors again. Good thing he had his school project to keep him busy at home.

Justice was actually glad to have time to add lots of details to his model of the reserve. It kept his mind away from the Shop 'n' Go incident, too. He really took care to make bushes and trees out of twigs he found and attached to a board with plasticine. Justice also spent a lot of time constructing little buildings out of tiny boxes and other materials he found around the house. He found out that he was pretty good at it and he took pleasure from Charity's and Mom's praise as his "reserve" took shape. Mom even bought him a paint set to use to make things the right colour. She let him use some of her cotton balls as snow – that way the "trees" didn't have to have leaves on them. In the end, Justice was pretty pleased with how his project was shaping up – now all he had to worry about was what he was going to say in front of his whole class.

chapter 12

Saturday finally arrived. The family was eating a quick breakfast in preparation to drive out to their reserve. Justice could hardly wait to get there. As he shoveled cereal into his mouth, he imagined his grandparents' house, the wide-open spaces around it and the bushes nearby where hideouts could be built.

"Justice, slow down, my boy," Mom chuckled. Her face had a slight smile on it and she looked more like her old self. "We'll get there in plenty of time."

At last they had their bags in the car and were preparing to drive away. Justice practically bounced in the back seat, praying their old car wouldn't give them any trouble on the highway.

The trip to the reserve was uneventful. As they passed fields that had been recently harvested and a few fenced-in pastures, Charity, as usual, chattered away about friends, school and whatever else was going on in her life. Mom, as usual, included Justice in the conversation when she could. Justice began to feel the events of the last while drift away with every kilometre the car drove.

As they entered the reserve, Justice's heart lifted further. There were so many familiar landmarks! The same old house stood near the road, its paint still peeling; the same little black dog came running out from another house, still barking; the same clumps of bushes were in the same great places for playing; and there was Kokum and Mushum's house ahead on the right! To Justice, approaching Kokum and Mushum's house was like coming home. His eyes hungrily took in the red shingles, slightly curled, the clean white siding with red trim and the shed where he and Mushum had spent hours working on fishing lines and rabbit snares. His heart raced as he anticipated getting into those bushes with some old pieces of wood for building or maybe chasing some gophers with his slingshot.

The car had barely rolled to a stop when Justice bounded out of it and raced up to the house. "Kokum! Mushum! We're here!" he called. Mom didn't even bother trying to tell him to be quieter. She just laughed as the arrival ritual repeated itself, the same as last time and many times before.

Kokum was waiting for them and came to the door, holding it open for the family. Her round face beamed at the children and their mother. "Heh, heh, look at you two, growing like weeds!" she teased.

"Hi, Mom." Mom grinned at her own mother. She reached out to Kokum and was embraced in a big hug and a kiss. "I'd love a cup of coffee," she admitted. "That drive isn't getting any shorter." Justice had already run through the tiny house as his mom sat down at the kitchen table and his grandma bustled around placing bannock, jam and plates on the table. A pot of hamburger soup waited on the stove. "Justice, my boy, come and eat something!" fussed Kokum. "You'll need all your energy to help Mushum." She turned to Charity. "How's my girl?" she asked, squeezing her in a hug.

"Good, Kokum," Charity responded quickly, her eyes shining. "Where *is* Mushum?"

"Oh, he's out in that shed of his, of course, still fiddling with that snowmobile. I think he likes being out there alone." Kokum chuckled.

"Can I go get him?" Charity asked, ready to run.

"Yeah, sure, tell him it's coffee time," the older woman answered immediately, then turned to her daughter and grandson. "How was the trip?"

"Oh, the usual. Nothing special," Mom responded. "I see they're rebuilding that gas station near the highway."

"Oh, yeah, the band council finally agreed to take it over and make something out of it. They're going to add a little grocery store, too," Kokum told her. "That'll be handy for Dad and me. I'll be glad not to drive into town just for milk or fruit."

"That's great!" Mom's voice glowed with interest. Justice hoped they weren't going to get into a whole discussion about the band council and all the decisions that needed to be made. It could take hours; the two women had many opinions about how the reserve should be run.

"What are you two gabbing about, eh?" exclaimed Mushum as he entered the house. "You just got here and you're yakking away. My ears are starting to hurt already." His eyes crinkled at the corners and Justice knew he was joking, as he did so often.

"Oh, you!" cried Kokum. "Never mind us, we've got a lot of catching up to do." She put her hands on Mom's shoulders. "I've missed my girl." She smiled down at Mom, and they hugged again.

Mushum held out his arms. "Justice, how are you?"

"I'm good, Mushum!" For the first time ever, Justice wasn't sure if he should hug his grandfather or shake his hand. Mushum decided for him, surrounding him with his big arms. Justice could smell Mushum's smell, a mixture of cigarette smoke, woodsmoke from his shed and soap. He closed his eyes a moment and breathed in deeply.

After a moment Mushum held Justice out at arm's length. "Well, look at you," he grinned, "you're getting to be a man."

Justice laughed. It was the same thing Mushum said every time he saw him but it still gave him a warm glow inside.

"And Charity," he said, "how's the prettiest girl in Monarch City?"

"Oh, Mushum!" Charity bubbled, "I'm fine!" And she ran to hug Mushum. *She sure doesn't worry about being too old to hug Mushum,* thought Justice.

"All right, you four, sit down and have coffee," Kokum urged. "The bannock's getting cold."

"Okay, but Justice and I are heading out to the shed right after coffee. Right, eh Jus?" His grandfather looked at him expectantly.

"Yup," Justice replied, reaching for the jam. "What are we going to work on?"

"Oh, that's man stuff." Mushum winked. "We can't tell these girls what we're doing out there."

Justice laughed. He knew Mushum would have something interesting for him to look at and learn about in the shed. He *could* tell his mom and sister all about it if he really wanted to, but it was a big deal between them that he and Mushum never did. He hurried through eating his bannock and a bowl of soup, so much so that his mom gave him a disapproving look, probably about the amount of food he had stuffed into his mouth at once.

Finally, Mushum was done his coffee, and they shrugged into their jackets and headed out the door for the shed. The pungent smell of woodsmoke surrounded Justice as he entered it. Mushum had an old wood stove burning in there whenever the temperature dropped below freezing.

MUSHUM'S SNOWMOBILE took up the entire space in the middle of the little building, its motor open with strange-looking parts laid out on the hood. Justice went right over and fingered one of the greasy motor pieces.

"Now don't forget, Jus," Mushum said, "I put each part in its own place so I can remember what it's for."

Justice was glad he hadn't moved anything. "So what's wrong with the motor, Mushum?" he asked.

"That's a good question, my boy. It doesn't work right," Mushum answered, grinning and raising his eyebrows at Justice. They laughed. Obviously, that's why he had taken the motor apart.

Mushum continued. "It seems to cough when it's running, and once at the end of last winter it died on me when I was out across the lake. Lucky thing I got it going again or it would've been a long walk home."

Wow, Justice thought, *the lake is outside of the reserve. That would've been a two- or three-hour walk home.* "We better get this thing fixed," he said.

"Well, now, I think these parts just need a little cleaning," Mushum explained. Mushum carefully unscrewed a spark plug with a special wrench, keeping back a little so Justice could see what he was doing. "See all this black carbon? That's got to come off." He scraped it carefully with a file.

Mushum nodded to Justice. "Why don't you try the next one?" Justice tried hard to remember what Mushum had done. He used the wrench on the next spark plug, looking to Mushum for a nod to make sure he was doing it right. "You're being careful, my boy," Mushum praised. Gently, Justice scraped the second plug, trying to get rid of all the carbon the way Mushum had. "Let's try that and see how she runs."

When everything was back in place, Mushum tried the motor and it started reluctantly.

"You did it!" Justice shouted.

Mushum smiled and turned off the engine. "*We* did it," he said.

Mushum straightened up a little, his hands on his lower back. "So how's school going, Justice?" he asked, stretching.

"Pretty good," Justice replied, wondering whether his mom had told Mushum about the Shop 'n' Go.

"You keeping out of trouble?"

Justice shot a quick look at his grandfather, but he seemed unaware of what had happened lately.

"Yeah, mostly," he replied evasively.

"Mostly, eh?" Mushum chuckled, waiting expectantly. "Does that mean, 'Not always'?"

"Well, you know, Mushum, no one's perfect." Justice squirmed. He wished they could change the topic.

Mushum gazed at him for a moment, then patted his pockets for his cigarettes. "You know, Jus, I used to fight a lot when I was in school." He paused to light his smoke. "I always wanted to be right and always had to prove it." Mushum chuckled and shook his head. "I proved my nose could bleed but I'm not sure what else I proved," he finished, a faraway look in his eyes.

There was silence as Justice searched for words to tell Mushum what had been going on. Finally he looked at Mushum, then down at his feet. "There's these kids that have been bugging me and Charity," he began. "I can't let them do that to us."

"Ah" Mushum sat down and leaned back on his old chair, nodding his head. "So you've been out to prove something too?"

Justice looked at the floor. Now that he was in front of Mushum he was ashamed that he had been fighting.

Mushum smiled at Justice. "You know, Jus, I knew some kids like that when I was young. They made me mad, but one day I looked at them really hard, trying to figure out why they picked on me. I saw that they weren't happy inside. They wanted me to feel that way, too."

"But why?" Justice cried, his voice shaking.

"I don't know," Mushum said. "They didn't tell me. But I started to get an idea."

"What was it?"

"You know how we're always taught to treat each other with respect?" Justice nodded. "I saw that they didn't respect me. Of course, I still didn't know why." Mushum got up and cleaned his hands with a rag, passing the rag to Justice for him to do the same.

"Did you figure it out?"

Mushum sat down again. "Think about those kids who came after you."

Justice thought about Trey and his friends. Maybe they were like the kids Mushum talked about. Unhappy inside. *What made a person feel happy? What made them feel bad?*

"Well," he said, "I feel good about myself if I do good things."

Mushum nodded and smiled. "What if you do bad things?"

Justice thought he might be starting to understand. Wanting to hurt Trey hadn't felt good.

"I guess they don't feel good about themselves," he said after a moment. "Maybe that's why they want to hurt other people."

"Maybe so," Mushum replied. "I suppose what matters is how *you* handle things."

"What do you mean?"

"In the end," Mushum went on, "we have to be responsible for how we treat other people. We're not asked to be proven right, we're asked to show respect." He paused. "Even if the other guy doesn't respect us – and that's hard."

Justice knew it was hard. He knew he wanted to pound some of those other kids, to make them take back what they had done and said. How could he walk away and ignore their taunts?

"So what do you think, Jus?" Mushum asked. "Can you respect people who don't show you respect?"

"I'll try, Mushum," he answered. He wanted to make Mushum proud but he wondered whether he really could do it.

chapter 13

Early the next morning, Justice was awakened by soft noises coming from the kitchen. When he tiptoed out to investigate, he found his grandfather quietly sipping coffee and putting bannock into a bread bag.

"Mushum?" he called in a low voice, "what are you doing?"

"Justice," Mushum spoke softly, motioning him over, "I'm going to visit Mr. Blackquill. You know, our neighbour?" Mushum nodded his head toward a nearby house.

Justice was surprised. Mr. Blackquill had always seemed crabby to him. *Why would Mushum want to go visit him?* "Why," he asked aloud, "is he sick?"

"Oh no, I just make it a habit to go see him once in a while. I thought everyone was still asleep." He paused. "Do you want to come with me?"

Justice didn't really want to go to see Mr. Blackquill. He usually went out of his way to avoid him and his house. Mushum waited for an answer.

"Yeah, sure," he replied, shrugging.

As THEY TRUDGED across the 400 metres or so separating the two houses, Mushum puffed on a smoke and pointed out the distant pond to Justice. "It never did get as full of water as usual this year," he told Justice. "I sure worry about the poor ducks who tried to nest there. Don't think they made out too good," he said, shaking his head sadly. Justice enjoyed hearing his grandfather talk about nature. Mushum seemed to know everything and he loved it all, almost as much as he loved Justice and Charity.

"Are the ducks still there, Mushum?" Justice asked, thinking about going over to have a look at them.

"Oh no, the winged ones are all gone south by now, my boy," Mushum told him. "They're too smart to stay here in winter." Soon they arrived at Mr. Blackquill's door. A broken window and sagging steps begged for someone to fix them up. Justice shoved his hands in his pockets and dragged behind his mushum, scuffing at some loose gravel by the door.

Mushum stamped his boots on the front step to let Mr. Blackquill know he was there. He opened the door slowly, revealing a dim room. "Floyd, it's Leon!" he called out. "Are you home?" There was a shuffling sound and an old man came to the door.

"Leon? What do you want? It's early." Mr. Blackquill asked hoarsely

"Oh, I know that, Floyd, but I knew you'd be up," Mushum chuckled. "How about some bannock? Pearl made it fresh yesterday."

Mr. Blackquill nodded to Justice and Mushum to come in. "Guess I could eat some bannock."

As Justice came further into Mr. Blackquill's house, he could see clutter everywhere. The kitchen table, the counter and even the couch were covered with papers, newspapers and plates of crumbs. A cat sat licking one of the plates by the kitchen sink. Justice cringed inwardly. This sure didn't look like his kokum and mushum's house!

"Well, where's this bannock?" Mr. Blackquill demanded.

"Oh, here, it's in a bread bag," Mushum answered, offering it to him.

"Hm. Looks good," Mr. Blackquill said. "So, who's this?" He looked harder at Justice. "You're not one of those kids who's been throwing rocks at my cats, eh?" His rough voice made Justice unsure what to say.

"Couldn't have been Justice here, Floyd. He lives in Monarch."

"Time was, kids respected the elders." He looked straight at Justice. "Do you respect your elders?"

Justice swallowed hard. "Yeah, I do," he said.

"Good thing, eh, Leon? He could be in trouble otherwise."

Justice squirmed where he stood, wishing Mr. Blackquill's attention was elsewhere. Mushum seemed to feel his discomfort.

"How about some coffee, Floyd?" Mushum said.

"Coffee, eh? I might have some around here." Mr. Blackquill shuffled over to the kitchen cupboards and pulled out a tin of coffee. Mushum went ahead and cleared himself a chair, placing the newspapers underneath it and a sock on top of the papers. He sat down comfortably, as though he did this all the time. Justice watched Mr. Blackquill measure out the coffee and set it to boil on the stove. He leaned against Mushum's chair.

Mushum settled back in his chair. "So how you been keeping?" he asked.

"Hold on a minute, I'll get there," responded Mr. Blackquill gruffly. "I'm looking for mugs." He rattled through several cupboards until he found two, eyeing them suspiciously. When the coffee boiled, he brought everything to the table and poured coffee for Mushum and himself. He seemed to have forgotten Justice.

Mushum took a sip of his coffee. "That's good," he said.

"Well, you asked how I'm doing, Leon," began Mr. Blackquill. He pulled a piece of bannock out of the bread bag. "Last week I went to see that doctor in the city." Mr. Blackquill waved his hand and shook his head as though he didn't think much of the doctor. For my back, eh?" he added. "It's giving me a lot of trouble. Ahhh, he doesn't know what to do about it. Some days it's hard just getting out of bed."

Mr. Blackquill took a sip of coffee. He bit into the bannock. "Say, that is good." He took another bite. "But what does that doctor know about back pain, real pain? He's young enough to be my grandson."

"I sure know how a bad back feels, Floyd," Mushum

said. I can't get under my snowmobile any more if I have something big to fix. Good thing I have Justice here, because he sure helps me." Mushum smiled at Justice. "When he's around, anyway. Getting old's not much fun, eh?" Mushum went on.

Mr. Blackquill chewed on his bannock thoughtfully. "You got that right, Leon." he replied. "Kokum Hawkfeather would have known which tea to brew that would have helped me," Mr. Blackquill said, nodding to himself. "And we respected our elders!" he added.

"Remember when *we* were young, Floyd? We used to raid old Kokum Hawkfeather's garden." Mushum chuckled. "She always wondered why that garden didn't produce so well."

Justice was amazed to hear that his grandfather had ever done anything wrong, besides the fighting he'd told him about earlier. He knew Mushum would never do that now.

"You know, I forgot we did that," Mr. Blackquill replied, leaning back in his chair. "Do you remember the wake they had when she died? I think that's the biggest one this reserve has ever seen."

"Yeah, everyone loved Kokum Hawkfeather," agreed Mushum. "And all those kids of hers have moved away now," he added, nodding his head, his eyes seeing events from the past.

"Yeah. Ten, I think she had." Mr. Blackquill seemed really interested in this story. "And not one of them on the reserve now."

"You know, I think some of them might live in Monarch City," Mushum commented, turning to Justice. "Jus, do you know any Hawkfeather kids?"

Mr. Blackquill, still chewing bannock, swung towards Justice, listening for the answer. His gaze on Justice made Justice's mouth go dry.

"Uh, I don't think so." He racked his brain to remember if he had ever heard that last name before.

"Ahhh, who knows where they live?" Mr. Blackquill waved his hand dismissively. "City's so big, they could be anywhere. Me, I like to know my neighbours."

"It's nice to see people you know at the store, too." Mushum agreed. "Did you hear that the band council is taking over the gas station and making it into a store?"

Mr. Blackquill had not heard this news and he and Mushum talked about it for quite a while as they sipped coffee. Justice couldn't believe how they could chat away like old buddies when Mr. Blackquill had been so miserable when they'd first arrived.

Finally Mushum stood up, offering his hand to Mr. Blackquill. "Well, Floyd, we better go. We still have work to do on that snowmobile and winter's coming."

Mr. Blackquill shook Mushum's hand. "I know it, Leon," he replied. "My bones say so."

Mushum laughed. "I remember the days when my bones didn't talk to me!" Mr. Blackquill laughed too, as Mushum and Justice headed out the door.

"See you next time, Floyd," Mushum said, nudging Justice to shake Mr. Blackquill's hand.

"Yeah, bye. And Justice," Mr. Blackquill put a finger up to give Justice directions, "tell your Kokum Pearl she still makes the best bannock around." Mr. Blackquill shut the door after them.

Mushum and Justice walked a little way in silence. Finally Justice burst out, "Mushum, why do you go visit him? He's so grouchy."

"Oh that." Mushum nodded his head. "That's why I go." Mushum smiled at Justice's puzzled look. "I've known him a long, long time, Justice. Mr. Blackquill doesn't have someone like Kokum to talk to every day like I do.

That's true, thought Justice. *Who would want to live there? That would be pretty lonely.*

"You see, his wife died a few years back," Mushum went on, "and ever since then he just doesn't like too many visitors. Unless I show up with Kokum's bannock. And of course, who doesn't like Kokum's bannock?" Mushum laughed teasingly. They were almost home. "Maybe we should have some ourselves, eh?"

Justice realized he was starving. "Yeah, let's have some right now!"

"Okay, but let's not wake up the girls," Mushum dropped his voice as they neared the house. "It'll be just us."

Justice felt warm inside, despite the chill in the air.

chapter 14

The rest of the weekend sped by and too soon Justice's family was saying goodbye. They hugged all around, with promises to call when they got home. Mom made sure that Mushum and Kokum would have their car looked at for winter before it snowed. It seemed funny that she was their kid, but she worried about them almost the same way she worried about him and Charity.

On the way home, Charity chatted about the friends she had seen while she was on the reserve. Every time they drove up, a group of girls seemed to materialize out of nowhere and Charity always had friends at the door. *Just like at home,* Justice thought. She spent a lot of time with Kokum, too. Justice was amazed at how she found cooking with their grandma fun. She seemed to think that everything Kokum did was great.

"...and she made muffins without eggs!" Charity was saying. "She put in a banana and they turned out fine!" Justice guessed that was something pretty amazing.

"Yeah, Kokum sure can make something out of almost nothing," Mom agreed. "That's what happens when you don't have a store close by. You learn to 'make do.'"

"She sure does 'make do,'" Charity agreed. "But she always has lots of flour on hand!" They all laughed. Kokum's bannock was famous on the reserve. Almost everyone made bannock, but no one made bannock like Kokum.

As they pulled into their driveway, Mom turned to the children. "How about tea and toast and then everyone gets to bed?" she suggested. "We're all tired, and there's school and work tomorrow."

"Sure!" Justice and Charity chimed in together. Mom didn't really need to ask; they always had tea and cinnamon toast when they got home from Kokum and Mushum's house. It was their ritual.

A few minutes later, the family was around the table in their cozy kitchen. Justice crunched into the buttered toast and savoured the hot tea. Even Charity was quiet as they enjoyed their snack.

"You brought home some bannock, right?" Justice asked his mom.

"Of course, Jus." Mom chuckled. "You can take it for lunch tomorrow."

"Oh, good," he sighed with relief.

"All right, you two, off to bed," Mom said, stifling a yawn. "Dishes in the sink."

Justice was happy to climb into bed. He'd had a busy day after getting up early and he fell asleep quickly, thinking about Mushum's kindness to Mr. Blackquill.

THIN, WINTRY SUNLIGHT struggled through his window when Justice awoke the next morning. The cold had settled in for good now and he could only hope for the first big snowfall to come soon. *Why is it harder to get up in winter?* he wondered.

Yawning and stretching, he thought again about Mushum's words: *Mr. Blackquill doesn't have someone like Kokum to talk to every day like I do.* Justice considered his own family as he pulled on his jeans. Yes, sometimes Charity chattered too much and his mom knew everything that went on. But if he needed someone to talk to, they *were* there for him.

Justice pulled a sweater out of a drawer. What if he didn't have anyone, like Mr. Blackquill? Would he be a bit grumpy, too? Justice couldn't imagine life without the others around. It made him wonder about Trey's family. What were they like? Justice knew he had a mom and some older brothers, but that was about all he knew.

Charity stuck her head into his room. "Jus, remember we have to start presenting our Canadian places projects today!"

Justice groaned. He didn't like having to talk in front of the class. Charity, of course, loved it and she flounced around in anticipation, holding out something she'd drawn.

"How do you like my picture of the CN Tower?" she asked, her eyes sparkling.

"Looks good!" he exclaimed, and he meant it. Charity *was* artistic and she had obviously spent time perfecting her final drawing.

Justice hoped his project was okay. He was proud of his model of the reserve, made out of small boxes and cans. He had spent a lot of time painting everything the right colours and had even made more bushes out of yarn and other materials Mr. Wilson had given him at school. But he wondered now if Charity was right – talking about the reserve might seem boring to some people. He shrugged inwardly. Too late now – the projects were done and due to be handed in today.

Less than an hour later, Justice and Charity had locked up, left their house and were trudging to school. As Justice approached the schoolyard, he could see Vance whipping through the monkey bars. He grinned at a really daring move but his smile quickly vanished as he scanned the rest of the playground.

Trey was already there. His dark head of hair stuck up above pretty much everyone else's, and, as usual, he seemed to be in the middle of turmoil. Justice sighed. He didn't really feel like meeting up with Trey again, especially if Trey was in the mood to cause problems. He was worried that something might happen to his project. Maybe he could just blend in unnoticed.

No such luck. When Trey caught sight of Justice, he

slipped out of the group and headed toward him. *What does he want now?* Justice thought.

"Pretty Boy," Trey spat out. "Haven't seen *you* around lately. Guess you've been busy playing with your little toys here."

Justice shrugged and tried to move around Trey. Another of Trey's "friends," a blond boy, was right there.

"Yeah, where've you been?" the blond-haired boy demanded.

"I dunno," Justice muttered and again tried to go around him.

Trey stepped right in front of him. "We asked you Where. You. Been." Trey punctuated each word with a shove on Justice's shoulder.

"I dunno, around, I guess." Justice heard his voice get louder and harsher and his heart pounded.

Surprisingly, Trey backed off a little. "Well, we all missed you," he sneered.

"Yeah, we *missed* you," echoed his buddy. He yanked one of the houses from Justice's model of the reserve. "This is what's gonna happen to you," he sneered as he crushed it in his hand.

"See you after school, Justice," Trey promised, his eyes narrowed and a menacing tone in his voice.

Great, Justice thought, *what does Trey have against me?*

chapter 15

Justice had a hard time keeping his mind on school work after Trey's threat. Charity presented her project and the class ate it up. She was so enthusiastic you couldn't help but be excited about Toronto just listening to her. And Justice was right; the other kids were impressed by her detailed drawing of the CN Tower. Justice was relieved to find out that his presentation would have to wait until the next day. But his joy over this news was quickly squashed by thoughts of Trey and his buddy, and the walk home after school. *What did Trey mean, "See you after school?"* Justice wondered. It certainly wasn't going to be anything positive. He hoped he could keep his distance.

"Justice, I asked you to hand out the newsletters," Mr. Wilson was saying, a puzzled look on his face. *Why didn't I hear him before?* Justice wondered as he took the papers from Mr. Wilson and began to pass them out.

Mrs. Lipswitch's voice crackled over the intercom. "Mr. Wilson, could you please send Trey to the office?"

At Mr. Wilson's nod, Trey got up and slouched non-chalantly to the door, as if it wasn't a big deal to be called down to the office. *Well, he's been there enough times, maybe it isn't a big deal,* Justice thought. He was glad that Trey was gone, even if it was only for a little while.

Too soon the school day was over and the children crowded out the classroom door and toward the stairs.

"See ya, Jimmy," Justice said, keeping an eye out for Trey. So far he hadn't seen him. *I can't believe he can do this to me,* he thought as he joined up with Charity, Vance and some other kids on their way out of the school.

Suddenly Justice remembered some notes he needed to go over for his presentation. "Charity, wait, I gotta run back into the classroom for something."

"Justice!" Charity groaned. "Can't you just leave it?"

"No, I need my notes," he replied, already pulling open the school door.

Justice bounded up the steps two at a time and rounded the corner into the hallway. The caretaker waved to him from the other end, but other than Mrs. McDonald, the hallway was deserted. It felt cool and calm in the school, not chaotic like when the kids were all there. Justice always liked the way the silence felt.

As Justice reached the classroom door, he heard adult voices inside. Mr. Wilson was talking to someone. Justice paused at the doorway, unsure whether or not to enter.

Mr. Baker was speaking. "A worker from Social Services was here to talk to Trey today."

So that's where Trey was this afternoon, thought Justice.

"Were they asking about the partying at his house?" asked Mr. Wilson. "Like I told you, he's been dead tired lately."

"I'm not sure about the details," Mr. Baker replied. "I know something went on there last weekend that they wanted to ask him about, but that's as much as I know."

"Well, I hope they keep an eye on things there," Mr. Wilson said. "I don't like what I'm seeing on this end. Trey can't keep his mind on his school work and he's getting to be a handful in the classroom."

How about on the street? Justice thought. *Or try being on the playground with him.*

Another teacher walked by. "Justice? Can I help you?" she asked him.

"Oh, yeah, no, I just need something from my classroom." Justice realized he had been eavesdropping. He entered the classroom as though he had just arrived in the school, trying not to look as though he had been listening.

"Justice? What brings you back? Missed me already?" Mr. Wilson teased.

"No, I forgot my notes," Justice mumbled. He usually liked to joke around with Mr. Wilson, but today he hastily grabbed what he needed and turned to leave. He couldn't wait to get out of the room. Justice felt as though Mr. Wilson would be able to tell by looking at him that he'd heard their conversation.

"Okay, see you tomorrow, Justice," Mr.Wilson said.

"Bye, Justice," Mr. Baker added.

"Bye," Justice called back over his shoulder. He relaxed again when he reached the hallway. He would have to think about what he had heard about Trey and his family. His home sure sounded different from Justice's own.

JUSTICE KEPT HIS THOUGHTS to himself as he rejoined Charity and the other kids outside. They were all teasing each other back and forth, and Charity was in the middle, as usual. Justice felt anger boil up inside him, knowing he couldn't be as carefree as they were. There was no way he could relax and joke around. He glanced over his shoulder again. No sign of Trey...yet.

As Justice and Charity left the schoolyard, Justice felt some of the tension seep away. Maybe Trey had been all talk today. He began to listen to Charity's stream of chatter. "So then I forgot what I was saying about the CN Tower, right when I was showing my drawing! Did you notice?" She peered anxiously into Justice's face. "Jus, could you tell?"

"No, no – it was fine," he said.

She seemed not to notice Justice's vague answer. "Well, that's good! I mean, if Mr. Wilson hadn't asked me some questions right then I would've been stuck." Justice could see her reliving the presentation in her mind. "Yeah, it's a good thing I kept going," she concluded.

"Yeah," Justice agreed absentmindedly.

"Chare! Jus!" Shaunie's voice cut off Charity's analysis. Shaunie was breathless as she caught up with the twins. "Hey, you guys, goin' home?"

"Yeah, I was just talking to Justice about my presentation," Charity responded.

"Charity, we were both *there,*" Shaunie chuckled, shaking her head.

"I know, but could you tell that –" Charity's question was cut off by a rough voice.

"Well, look who it is."

Trey. He and the blond boy were suddenly right behind them. Justice's heart began to race.

Justice, Charity and Shaunie glanced at each other. "Let's just go home," Justice said quietly. All three turned to walk away.

"Whaddya think you're doing, Pretty Boy?" Trey obviously wasn't going to let them go. "Taking those two with you, eh?"

His already racing heart began to gallop and Justice felt his face burn. He knew Trey was trying to make him mad. *What had Mushum said about people who were unhappy inside?* He knew Trey was one of those people, but he had no business bugging them!

"Look, Pretty Boy, I'm talkin' to you!" Trey shoved Justice from behind, pushing him off balance. He stumbled but stayed on his feet.

"Just leave us alone, Trey." Justice tried to sound final as he backed away, but his voice came out weak and unsure.

"I don't *think* so, Pretty Boy," Trey snapped, keeping up with Justice and cutting him off from the others. "You and your little girlfriend bug me," he continued, his teeth clenched, "and there's no Ms. Fayant here to save your hide this time!"

Justice couldn't think what to do. Trey was right – there *were* no adults around now. It was just Trey and his friend, and Justice and the girls. Trey moved in even closer.

"You better keep outta my way from now on," Trey was saying.

Justice hid his fear with a scoff. "Whatever," he shrugged, trying once again to step around Trey.

That set Trey off and he shoved Justice again, hard this time. Justice flew backwards off his feet and landed on his back with a jarring *thump*. For a few seconds he saw Trey through a kind of red haze as he struggled to get his wind back. Trey was saying something, but Justice couldn't quite make it out. Charity and Shaunie were yelling, but he couldn't tell what they were saying either.

No sooner was Justice on his feet than Trey was rushing at him, fire in his eyes. Before he could get away, Trey had his collar and threw him down again. Justice tried to keep his wits about him, and as Trey swung a fist at him, Justice instinctively snapped his foot forward, catching Trey in the stomach.

Taken by surprise, Trey doubled over in pain. Using this chance to stand up, Justice made no move to leave now, but stepped toward Trey, fingers clenched into fists. Suddenly he was grabbed from behind. Trey's friend! Justice had forgotten he was there. As Justice struggled to free himself from the other boy's grasp, Trey straightened up and, seeing Justice held captive, regained his sneer and swagger.

Justice tore free just as Trey came at him, fists flying. Justice tried to block the blows, but Trey was bigger and Justice wasn't used to fighting. Several times Trey's heavy fist plowed Justice hard in the head and stomach. With his arms shielding his face, Justice never really had the chance to make any solid hits of his own.

Finally, Trey took one last swing at Justice, striking him full on the side of his head. Justice dropped to the ground, his ear ringing. By this time, Charity and Shaunie's cries had brought a couple of neighbours out of their homes. Trey glanced around as a few adults began to gather and quickly motioned to his friend. In an instant they had disappeared down an alley.

Justice lay motionless on the sidewalk.

Chapter 16

Charity and Shaunie hurried over to Justice. Charity was crying.

"Justice, are you okay? You're bleeding!"

Justice got up slowly, muttering under his breath. He felt dizzy and confused. Blood dripped from his nose onto his jacket. He wiped at his nose with his hand, spitting blood out into the dirt by the sidewalk.

"Come on, we better get home," his sister said as she and Shaunie helped him up.

"Take this," said an older woman, thrusting a dishtowel into Justice's hand.

"Thanks," he mumbled. He held it up to his nose and slowly began walking in the direction of home.

Shaunie had been silent until now. "I'm scared of Trey!" she burst out. "Jus, he could've *killed* you!" Her voice shook and her eyes were filled with tears. "What are we gonna *do?*"

"Nothing," Justice spat. "We can't do a thing."

"Jus," argued Charity, "this is getting serious. You better tell Mr. Baker or at least tell Mom what's going on."

"No way! If we tell, it'll only be worse the next time. They'll get Trey into trouble and then he'll come after me again. I don't want him to have another reason to hate me."

They walked along in silence. Justice still held the towel to his face, although the nosebleed had mostly stopped. He hadn't realized how dangerous Trey really was. *So much for ignoring unhappy people,* he thought. *I guess they can make me pretty unhappy, too.* Justice had tried to do the right thing, but it sure hadn't turned out right for him.

"Jus," Charity turned to him again, "couldn't you tell Mom what happened but ask her to promise not to tell Mr. Baker who it was?" she suggested. "'Cause if *he* finds out it was Trey and Trey gets in trouble, then yeah, Trey's gonna get you worse next time!" Her voice rose in fear at that last thought.

"I dunno," Justice mumbled, "maybe."

Justice and Charity turned down the street before theirs to walk Shaunie home. As they said goodbye at her front walk, Shaunie gave Justice a wan smile and lifted her fingers in a half-hearted wave. "I hope you're okay, Jus."

"Yeah, thanks," he muttered as he watched her run up to her house.

"Justice, what are we gonna do about Trey?" Charity began again as soon as Shaunie was out of sight.

"I gotta think about it," Justice replied. "Mushum said to ignore him, but that doesn't work."

"You can't fight him again, Jus, he's too big and strong!"

Justice didn't reply. He knew Charity was right but he had no answer.

As CHARITY HELPED JUSTICE clean up his face from the nosebleed and cut cheek, they discussed what they might do about Trey.

"You've gotta tell Mom something, Jus," Charity pointed out. "For one thing, she's gonna want to know what happened to you!"

"I know, I know," said Justice, as though stopping Charity from saying it would make it false. "I just don't know if she'll get it that she can't tell Mr. Baker."

"Mom will understand, Justice," reasoned Charity. "She knows what it's like."

"No, she doesn't," Justice argued. "She's a grown-up and they think they can talk kids out of anything." Even as Justice said this, though, he remembered the conversation he had overheard between his mom and that person on the phone after swimming that time. She cared and was trying to get the other person to talk to someone but she didn't force it when that person was another adult. *Would she be the same with me?* he wondered.

While Justice and Charity got out the last of the bannock and some juice to snack on, they continued arguing about their dilemma. At first Justice was annoyed that Charity seemed to be interfering. Finally, though, he began to relax enough to realize that his family was there to help him and probably wouldn't do things to make it worse. At least, they'd try hard not to.

As MOM ENTERED the house after work, Justice met her at the door. "Justice, what happened to you? Are you all right?" she exclaimed, dropping her purse instantly.

"Mom, I have to talk to you," Justice said. He walked over to the couch. Mom was right behind him and sat down with him. Charity's concerned face hovered beside Mom's.

Mom waited for Justice to start. She wrung her hands and looked from one child to the other.

"Mom, I haven't told you everything that's been going on," Justice began. He met his mom's worried look with a quick glance. "There's been someone bugging us at school. He beat me up today." Mom started to say something, but Justice interrupted. "I can't tell you who it is, Mom, so don't even ask.

"I know you're gonna be mad at me, but there's nothing we can do about it. I just wanted to tell you the truth." Just saying that lifted a weight from Justice's shoulders that he hadn't even known he'd been carrying.

"Oh Jus, how long has this been going on? I wish you'd told me sooner!" Mom's face was pinched with worry and she had tears in her eyes when she put her arm around him.

Justice felt his mom's concern and care. "It's been going on a while, but I never told you before because I was afraid you would tell somebody."

Mom hugged Justice and they leaned back into the couch. Charity cuddled in next to them. Mom seemed to be thinking about something.

"Jus, I can understand that you don't want me to know who this is but I think we should let Mr. Baker know what's going on," Mom began. "He needs to put a stop to this, starting at school."

"But Mom, that's the whole problem, it's not just at school! And Mr. Baker getting after this kid will just make him madder at me." Justice's voice went up with the panic he was beginning to feel at Mom's suggestion.

"Won't you at least let me tell Mr. Baker what's happened? He should know this is a problem at school, too."

"No, I don't want this kid to get madder at me!"

"Well, Jus, I can't promise that I won't at least talk to Mr. Baker. Let me think it over, okay?"

chapter 17

By the next morning, Justice's head hurt in many places, he had bruises on his cheeks and his nose was too sensitive to touch. Just great! Today was the day Justice was supposed to give his presentation! *How am I gonna stand up in front of everyone looking like this?* He wanted to escape but headed for the shower anyway.

As the warm water ran over him, he remembered his mom's reaction to his injuries. She had been very upset, but although he had told her in the end that it was Trey he had fought, he made her promise not to tell Mr. Baker. He made Charity promise not to tell either. If his mom phoned the school about Trey, Trey's anger and fighting would only get worse.

As he sat down at the table, Mom sat down with him, which was unusual for her. Most days she was busy making lunches while he and Charity ate breakfast.

"You know, Justice, what happened to you reminds me of something that happened to me when I was in school. There was this girl – Cynthia – and she was always angry. She was mad at the teachers, she had fights on the playground – just mad. One day she and her two mean friends started bugging me after school. They called me names and put down my friends."

"Why?" Justice interrupted, unable to help himself.

"I thought Cynthia hated me but I never knew why. They did it again a few days later and then again. Pretty soon I was always on the watch for Cynthia. Sometimes I didn't see her after school but I never knew when I would."

By this time, Justice had stopped eating to listen.

"Some days I didn't want to go to school. Kokum and Mushum didn't know *what* was wrong. I had always loved school! They even took me to a doctor in Monarch City once because they thought I was sick too much!"

Justice nodded his head. He sometimes felt like missing school to avoid Trey, too.

"Then this one day I tried to play sick, but Kokum wouldn't let me. She said she was sure I was fine, no fever, no throwing up, and she kinda pushed me out the door to school. I had to run 'cause I was almost late by then. When I got close to school, I saw this Cynthia girl and she was bugging *someone else!* A younger girl! I couldn't believe it! I didn't know there was anyone else having the same problem as me!"

Just like Shaunie! Justice thought.

"Well, this other kid kinda took it for a while, then she did the strangest thing. She just stood right up to

Cynthia and said, 'Cynthia, you're not bugging me anymore.' Then she spotted me and said, 'Me and Margaret want you to leave us alone. Now beat it!'

"And you know what? Cynthia *did* leave the two of us alone after that. Oh, she was always in trouble as long as I knew her but she stopped coming after me. That's when I realized that Cynthia always picked on someone younger than her, or someone scared. She never came after anyone older, or someone who could fight.

"Justice," she tried again, "please let me tell Mr. Baker who was fighting you."

Charity squirmed in her chair. She didn't like conflict with Mom either but she understood how Justice felt; she hadn't told Mom that it was Trey and his friends who had pushed her around on the way back to school from Open Kitchen.

"Mom," Justice groaned, "don't ask me anymore."

"But honey, we should report this to Mr. Baker. The school should know what's going on!"

"I can handle it," Justice replied, trying to convince himself. *I wonder if she believes me?*

JUSTICE'S QUESTION was answered later that morning when Mr. Baker called several classes together in the gym. He talked about bullying and fighting in the schoolyard, as well as on the way to and from school. Mr. Baker mentioned some of the things that Mom had said. *Had Mom called Mr. Baker after all? What had she told him?*

"Bullies hurt your mind and feelings as well as your body. Everyone should feel safe at school and be able to tell me or any of the school staff about bullying that might be going on.

"Bullies hurt us all, even if we're not the ones being bullied. They make our school and our neighbourhood a scary place when it should be safe. They stop us from being ourselves, and learning and doing what we need to do."

Justice could feel his ears burning during this lecture, and he tried to look unconcerned and detached from the message.

"Bullies are usually people who are hurting inside." The room grew very quiet at this point. "It's hard to feel good about yourself when people don't like you, isn't it?

"It is up to the adults in your life to help you if you are in any kind of trouble. Bullying is one of the kinds of trouble you might experience," Mr. Baker explained.

Justice stole a glance back at Trey, only to be met by a furious glare. That seemed like a bad sign to Justice and he had trouble concentrating on Mr. Baker after that.

RIGHT AFTER LUNCH, it was time for the kids' presentations. Justice's name was drawn to go fourth. *How am I gonna wait that long?* he wondered. He hardly heard a word anyone else said in their presentations, even though he was supposed to be writing down questions to ask them.

Too soon, it was Justice's turn. The front of the classroom seemed miles away as he walked up to it, retrieved his model of the reserve from where it was on display on the side counter of the classroom and prepared to talk. The kids were a bit restless as he was about to begin and Mr. Wilson made Justice wait a moment while he settled them down. As he looked over his model before beginning, Justice was glad he'd spent a lot of time on it because of how realistic it looked now. He had even managed to cover up the damage Trey's buddy had done. He could almost see Kokum and Mushum working around their tiny yard beside their tiny painted box house.

Finally Mr. Wilson gave Justice the signal to start. As Justice began to tell about his reserve, Jimmy, who was wiggling around in his back row seat as usual, called out, "Hey, that's near *my* reserve!"

"Yes, Jimmy, it is, but it's Justice's turn to talk now," reprimanded Mr. Wilson. Jimmy settled back into his desk somewhat, but Justice was encouraged by Jimmy's interest.

"How many of you have a special place where you love to go, and you really do get to go there?" Justice asked the group. He glanced around, ignoring Trey's menacing scowl as best he could. Many of the other children had raised their hands, a few offering their ideas out loud.

Justice spoke over them. "Well, my reserve is my special place and here's why. When I go there, I can run free outside. Me and my friends – I mean, my friends and I – even build hideouts in the bushes. I've hunted rabbits there and I've been fishing," Justice said proudly. He stood a little taller and spoke in a strong, clear voice about the place he loved.

The kids were all listening now, and Mr. Wilson was nodding his head and taking notes. "The best thing about my reserve is that my kokum and mushum live there," Justice continued.

There was a sneer from Trey. "Kokum and Mushum, who says that?" Several kids around Trey shushed him loudly.

Justice pushed Trey out of his mind and concentrated on the interested children. "My mushum lets me help him fix his snowmobile and he lets me drive it, too." A few of the students *oohed* in an impressed way.

Justice realized that a lot of them didn't get to do that, so he added, "I've even made my own rabbit snare and it worked." Everyone looked impressed at this, even Mr. Wilson.

The rest of Justice's talk breezed by – he hardly remembered what he said. It felt as though he was sailing on a cloud, once he realized that the kids *were* interested. *I never even forgot what to say.* He couldn't believe he could actually do this. Maybe other kids *did* want to hear about the reserve. He couldn't wait to tell Mom, Mushum and Kokum how well he had done.

"Jus!" Charity appeared beside him as he gathered his belongings at the end of the school day. "You did a great job! You even said extra stuff I never heard before – you're brave!"

"Good job, Justice," added Mr. Wilson's voice. "Thank you for reminding us all that special places don't have to be far away and exotic."

"Thanks." Justice flushed again with pride.

Mr. Wilson paused. "Do you visit your kokum and mushum often? You know – you're lucky to have them."

"Well, we don't go out there too much but we just went a few weeks ago," Justice replied. "That's when Mushum and I were working on the snowmobile."

"Well, good for you for remembering your roots." Mr. Wilson went on. "I should get out to see my family one of these days, too," he mused. "Anyway, well done – you didn't seem nervous at all."

Justice almost laughed out loud. *Didn't seem nervous? I wish! I can't believe I pulled it off!* Justice couldn't stop grinning.

JUSTICE'S LIGHTHEARTED FEELINGS didn't last long.

He had been right to be worried during Mr. Baker's bullying lecture in the gym. Justice had just headed out the school doors to go home when Trey and a couple of his buddies came away from the monkey bars and strode straight toward Justice.

chapter 18

Listen, wuss, you better stop yapping to everyone before we get in a lot of trouble. Haven't you got the message yet?" Trey seemed even angrier than usual and a sick feeling curdled in Justice's gut. He noticed a small crowd gathering around him and Trey.

Am I going to run away forever? When's this gonna stop? Justice glanced around, grateful to see Charity, Vance, Shaunie and a few other friends from his class. He felt braver with them standing behind him. Even Jimmy was there.

"No, Trey," he said and the strength in his voice surprised him. "The only message I get is that you're not gonna push me around anymore."

Trey opened his mouth as though about to say something, but Justice turned to walk away. Trey shoved him from behind.

"You're not walking away, wuss!" he yelled.

"Yeah, I am," Justice answered, his voice hardly

shaking. "I *am* walking away." And with that, he did. His friends followed.

"You'll regret that, Stoneyplain!" Trey screamed after him. "You won't always have your girlfriends around to protect you!"

Justice ignored him and kept walking, although his legs felt like jelly and his heart was racing. As the distance between him and Trey increased, a few of the other kids slapped him on the back.

"Way to go, Jus!" Vance called.

"That's telling him!" said another.

"He can't scare us," a third bravely chimed in.

Charity and Shaunie joined Justice, smiling to themselves. The group continued down the street, congratulating Justice and each other. Justice smiled but wondered inwardly what *would* happen the next time.

THE KIDS WERE BUZZING with gossip the next day at school. Trey wasn't there, but no one knew for sure why. There were rumours about a big party at Trey's.

"I heard that there were eight cop cars at Trey's house!" one girl claimed.

"We live down the street," reported another, "and we heard sirens for a long time in the middle of the night."

"I heard they took Trey's brother to jail again," a third kid told everyone.

"No way, Jason. They won't take him to jail just for a party," someone else said.

The talk continued this way until the bell rang and the kids lined up to go into school.

JUSTICE RELAXED A LITTLE as Mr. Wilson took attendance. When he got to Trey's name, he paused and said, almost to himself, "Oh yeah, Trey won't be here for a few days." He marked that in the attendance book accordingly.

Won't be here for a few days? Justice wondered. *What does that mean? Maybe he went to jail.*

Justice suddenly heard Mushum's words again, about unhappy people trying to make you unhappy, too. Justice thought maybe Mr. Blackquill was in that group. Maybe Trey was, too. Justice wondered for about the hundredth time what it was that made Trey hate him so much. Maybe it wasn't really Justice's fault at all?

"Mr. Blackquill doesn't have someone like Kokum to talk to every day like I do," Mushum had said. Did Trey have anyone to talk to? *All he knows is fighting.* Justice remembered again that his own family was always around for him, even if sometimes he thought they were around too much.

Justice thought more about his conversation with Mushum the night before. "Justice," he had cheered, "I knew you could do a great presentation! Did you mention your old mushum?" His words had a chuckle in them.

"Actually, I did, Mushum," Justice had answered his grandfather. "I told everyone how you taught me to make rabbit snares and fix the snowmobile."

Mushum had been quiet for so long Justice had thought maybe they'd been cut off. "Mushum?"

"You make your mushum proud, my boy," he finally said. "You'll be a good man one day."

Justice's memories were interrupted by Mr. Wilson handing out the morning's assignment.

BY THE END OF THE WEEK, Trey was back in school. He was acting a little differently, though. For one thing, he'd had a haircut and was sporting a new backpack. It was cool, with shimmery neon colours. Justice wondered what was going on.

As the kids streamed out of school for recess, Justice was jostled into Trey. "Watch it, Stoneyplain," he growled, his hands balling up into fists.

Justice braced himself for what would come next, but Trey turned back to his buddy and continued talking. "So I'll give you the number where I'm staying. It's called Davis House."

That's it – "Watch it?" Justice wondered.

Trey's friend, the blond boy, raised his eyebrows and his eyes widened in recognition. "My brother was at Davis House for a while!" he exclaimed. "They're really strict."

"Yeah, but they're okay," Trey answered with a shrug.

Wow, what a change, Justice thought as he turned towards the monkey bars. *Maybe Trey will be safe from any gangs while he's there.* He wondered what made Trey ignore him, but was grateful that he did.

"Hey, Shaunie," Justice called to her across the playground. "Wanna walk home with us today?"

"Sure," Shaunie replied, a small smile edging across her face.

"Great," Justice answered back warmly, having nothing else to say to her, as usual. He chuckled to himself. *I guess not everything changes,* he thought. *One day I'm gonna think up something to say to her. Maybe Mushum has some ideas.*

He ran to the monkey bars, where Vance swung, doing his usual ape routine. "Hey, Justice!" he called. "Come on up!"

*L*ori Saigeon is an elementary school teacher, living and working in Regina, Saskatchewan. It was while teaching in inner-city Regina that Lori noticed a lack of fiction geared for urban children, particularly those growing up in a small prairie city and most especially those with a First Nations/Metis background.

Lori has been a teacher for over 24 years. She achieved her Master of Education from the University of Regina and published a handbook, *Inviting Writing into the Science Classroom: How Teachers Open the Door. Fight for Justice* is her first work of fiction.

Born and raised in Regina, Lori has been writing since she was a child – her first book-length story, "The Flying Mouse," was written in grade 6. Lori is married and is continually inspired by her three wonderful, school-age children.

ENVIRONMENTAL BENEFITS STATEMENT

Coteau Books saved the following resources by printing the pages of this book on chlorine free paper made with 100% post-consumer waste.

TREES	WATER	SOLID WASTE	GREENHOUSE GASES
12 FULLY GROWN	**5,509** GALLONS	**334** POUNDS	**1,144** POUNDS

Calculations based on research by Environmental Defense and the Paper Task Force. Manufactured at Friesens Corporation